BARN DANCE

BARN DANCE

A Novel

Chuck Brown

iUniverse, Inc.
New York Lincoln Shanghai

BARN DANCE

Copyright © 2006 by Chuck Brown

iUniverse books may be ordered through booksellers or by contacting:

iUniverse
2021 Pine Lake Road, Suite 100
Lincoln, NE 68512
www.iuniverse.com
1-800-Authors (1-800-288-4677)

ISBN-13: 978-0-595-40967-9 (pbk)
ISBN-13: 978-0-595-85325-0 (ebk)
ISBN-10: 0-595-40967-9 (pbk)
ISBN-10: 0-595-85325-0 (ebk)

Printed in the United States of America

For Pat,
and the dance goes on.

CHAPTER 1

▼

Gabby didn't talk much. His nickname derived from Gabriel, not from a talkative nature, and although some attributed his reticence to shyness, others pointed to the fact that he lived alone and simply had no one with whom to converse. Still others saw a connection between the shyness and the living alone, but whatever the root cause, Gabby didn't talk much.

Born Gabriel Cox, the only child of Elton and Martha Cox, Gabby lived the first thirty-six years of his life with his parents on the Cox family farm, six miles east of Hayesboro, Minnesota. Now at forty, he was still on the farm, but alone since the sudden death of his parents in a car crash four years earlier. Restocking the family never occurred to Gabby. For thirty-six years there had been three of them, and that had always seemed just right. Now, for reasons beyond his control, the family was down to one, and because a smaller number was less likely to draw attention, that seemed about right too. Gabby was wary of the world, and the world, in an apparent spirit of cooperation, pretty much ignored Gabby, that is until the day the world crashed into his life.

*　　　*　　　*　　　*

It was a warm July morning. The corn was fully tasseled, and the air was sweet with its pollen, hinting at abundance to come, and Gabby was in the barn doing pig chores. He didn't think of himself as a pig farmer. To be a real pig farmer these days you had to raise them by the thousand and col-lect their shit in stinking lagoons that poisoned the ground water and sick-ened the neighbors. No, Gabby was no modern-day pig farmer; he raised cash crops of corn and soybeans and wheat, but each year he also raised a dozen or so pigs because it reminded him of how farming had been. Besides, he liked pork.

The pigs had been fed, and Gabby was filling the stock tank with water when the sound of an airplane rose above the squeals and snorts in the barn. In the next moment the noise grew loud enough to drown out the pigs, and in the moment after that, the sound became a deafening roar. Gabby looked to the ceiling, fully expecting a plane to explode through the roof. "*Yeeeeeee!*" it came, and then suddenly "*Yummm!*" as the plane roared close overhead and the sound receded. Gabby breathed a sigh of relief, but then he shook his head. The damage had been done. The pigs had stopped feeding and now were wedged tightly in a corner of the pen amid a frenzy of snorting.

"Goddamn Slade Walters," muttered Gabby. "How the hell's a man supposed to fatten panicked pigs?"

Slade Walters was a hotshot crop duster who flew his plane from an alfalfa field on his father's farm the next section over. Slade wasn't yet twenty-five, and Gabby was quite certain that he wouldn't reach thirty, but in the meantime his comings and goings too often took him low over Gabby's farm, scaring the pigs and generally disturbing the peace. Gabby had complained often, but to no avail, so he shrugged and turned back to his chores just as the growing roar of an airplane engine sounded through the barn walls again.

"Son-of-a-bitch!" Gabby yelled and raced for the door. Coming and going was one thing, but repeated dive-bombing was something else. This was getting personal. Out in the yard he looked skyward, wishing he had his twelve-gauge shotgun, but then his eyes widened with shock. It wasn't Slade Walters. It wasn't a crop duster.

It was a sleek twin-engine plane, the sort Gabby had seen on the news flying business bigwigs and politicians around the country. It came in low over the grove. Gabby waved his arms. It seemed a futile gesture, but to his surprise the pilot waggled the wings as the plane shot overhead, clearing the barn by no more than fifty feet.

The plane climbed and banked, and Gabby glimpsed long blond hair in the cockpit. Nothing else registered, but in that instant long blond hair was fixed in his brain. He watched as the plane continued its climbing turn, and then, to his astonishment, it dropped its nose and lined up for another run.

Who is this mad man? Gabby wondered. *And why's he buzzing my farm?*

He waved his arms again, but the plane came on, lower and lower. Gabby waved harder, but still it came, and there was no answering wing waggle now.

It was the big cottonwood tree. That's what they determined later. It stood some twenty feet above the rest of the grove, and as the plane roared in, its left wing clipped the very top of the tree. From Gabby's vantage point, it seemed to have little effect. There was no sound of contact to be heard over the engines' roar, and only a few leaves scattered. But then the plane shuddered and its right wing dipped. In the next instant, it crashed into Gabby's barn and exploded into a ball of fire.

CHAPTER 2

▼

The warm July morning had given way to a hot July afternoon, and Gabby watched from the shade of his porch as the ambulance drove slowly from the yard. There were no flashing lights or sirens. There was no hurry.

The porch ran the length of two sides of the house, providing access to the kitchen along one side and the living room along the other. The house itself was small and unpretentious, with only two bedrooms upstairs. The big porch with its post-supported roof was the only distinctive feature, and Gabby now sat on the steps of the kitchen side because it offered the best shade from the afternoon sun. His elbows rested on his knees and his chin rested on his hands as he glumly surveyed the scene.

Across the yard and to his right, framed against a cornfield, stood the newest structure on the farm: a steel pole building that Elton Cox had built the year before he died. It housed the tractor and the combine and as many of the farm's implements as could be wedged inside. Its steel sides were light brown in color, a contrast to the white paint that adorned every other building on the place. To the left of the pole building was an old wooden granary that hadn't been used in years. Its paint was checked and flaking, and it leaned toward the pole building as if to indicate the prevailing wind. Next to the granary stood a small tool shed. Its paint was checked and flaking too, and it leaned in the direction opposite that of the granary. The tool shed had been the second-oldest building on the farm. Now it was the oldest, and Gabby's gaze continued to the left, to the charred and smoking ruins of what had been the oldest building until that morning.

It had been a good barn, built to last, and three generations of Coxes had maintained it well. More than any of the other buildings, the barn had stood for the family's roots and values, a reassuring permanence framed against the grove that had been Gabby's first sight each morning as he walked from the house to do chores. Now it was a tangle of blackened timbers with an airplane rudder rising from its midst. The wind was light, but the occasional stirring wafted smoke toward Gabby, smoke that carried a hint of roast pork.

Sam Stack slowly crossed the yard, approaching the house. Sam was the county sheriff, and he, along with a deputy, had been the first to arrive after Gabby called 9-1-1. The Hayesboro Volunteer Fire Department had arrived three minutes after the sheriff, with the Hayesboro ambulance following close behind. Forty minutes after that, the first helicopter appeared. "Channel 5" was painted on its fuselage. Channel 4 arrived six minutes later. The helicopters circled and hovered, fanning smoke in every direction as Sam Stack angrily tried to wave them off.

At eleven in the morning, two hours after the crash, the third helicopter arrived. It was larger than the first two and it didn't bother with circling or hovering. It swooped in over the grove and landed with authority in the middle of the yard. Dust still billowed beneath its rotors as the door slid open and six men climbed out. Each man wore a dark blue nylon windbreaker with "NTSB" printed across the back and a dark blue ball cap bearing the same initials. The men in blue immediately started barking orders at everyone: the firemen, the sheriff, the deputy, and even Gabby when he approached the man in blue giving most of the orders. Gabby had questions, naturally, and as the property owner, he thought he was entitled to answers. As it turned out, he wasn't. He was ordered back and told to stay out of the way. Now as the firemen stowed their gear and prepared to leave, the men in blue roamed through the charred ruins and the surrounding yard, marking scattered bits of airplane with little blue flags. The dark blue windbreakers had all been shed in the midday heat, revealing light blue polo shirts, again bearing the letters NTSB.

Sam Stack came to a stop in front of Gabby. He was tall and broad-shouldered with the beginnings of a gut bulging slightly over his belt. His dark blue ball cap said "Sheriff," and aviator-style sunglasses added to the impassive expression that usually graced his face. The epaulets on his uniform shirt were brown to match his pants. The shirt itself was khaki and stained with sweat at the armpits and where his belly pressed against it. He sighed as his hand came to rest on his holstered gun. "Helluva mess, huh, Gabby?"

Gabby nodded, pondering the mess and the men in blue crawling through it. "Who are those guys anyway? Some kinda state cops?"

Sam shook his head. "They're feds. National Transportation Safety Board."

"They're kinda pushy."

"Like I said, Gabby, they're feds. They think they're the boss of everyone." Sam nodded toward the men in blue. "These particular guys are sorta like the FBI of plane crashes."

"So how long they gonna be here?"

Sam shrugged. "As long as they want, I reckon."

Gabby stared glumly. It didn't seem fair that a man who'd just lost his barn should have to put up with feds too, but his indignation turned quickly to shame. Someone had died, after all. "They got any idea who he was?"

"Not he—they," Sam corrected. "There were two of 'em."

Gabby shook his head, his shame now doubled. "So who were they?"

"Feds haven't seen fit to tell me yet, though I'm sure they've got a pretty good idea based on the plane's registration number."

Gabby stared at the smoking wreck. "Did you get close enough to…see inside?"

Sam nodded. "Yeah, I got a pretty good look before the feds got here. Had to make sure there weren't any survivors. Didn't expect any, of course, not in a mess like that, but a fella's gotta look."

"Burnt pretty bad, I s'pose."

Sam nodded again.

"Two guys, huh?"

"Actually, a man and a woman."

Gabby looked up, surprised. "You could tell?"

"Yeah. Easily. See, that's the strange thing, Gabby. They were naked."

"Jesus! Their clothes burnt right off 'em, huh?"

Sam paused. "I don't think so, Gabby. There were burnt remnants of clothing and shoes, but they were lying on the floor behind the seats. Way I see it, they were flying naked."

Gabby felt the weight of the day grow. He'd been having enough trouble getting his mind around everything else that'd happened, and now flying naked people? He stretched his imagination to fit this strange new piece into the puzzle. "I reckon it is pretty hot today."

Sam smirked. "Somehow I don't think they were trying to keep cool."

Gabby settled his chin glumly on his hands again, trying to sort through it all. He looked up as one of the feds approached the porch. The man had thin sandy hair and his blue polo shirt was sweat-stained like the sheriff's. He was the one who appeared to be in charge, the one who'd ordered Gabby back from the scene earlier. He was short, the top of his head coming level with Sam Stack's shoulder, but his small stature did nothing to diminish his air of authority.

He came to a stop in front of Gabby and consulted a clipboard that he carried in his left hand. "Mr. Cox?"

Gabby stood as if he'd been called to attention. "That's me."

"Mr. Cox, I'm Howard Blake with the National Transportation Safety Board. I'm in charge of this crash scene investigation, and I need to ask you some questions."

Gabby shrugged. "Sure." Then he asked a question of his own. "How long you fellas figure to be here?"

The fed eyed Gabby for a moment, and then he ignored the question. "Mr. Cox, I want you to tell me in your own words everything that happened."

Gabby felt an odd mix of anger and apprehension: anger at the fed's disregard for his rights as a property owner and apprehension at the niggling notion that he was being questioned as if he were somehow responsible for the crash. "Not much to tell," he said. "This fella came along and buzzed the farm a couple times, then on the third time he crashed into my barn."

The fed shook his head. "No, Mr. Cox, I need details. I want to know what you were doing at the time. I want to know everything you saw, even if you don't think it's important."

Gabby's dislike for the fed grew, but in spite of that he found himself complying with the fed's order. He described in detail doing chores. He told of the airplane buzzing the barn and of how it frightened the pigs. He told of how he'd thought it was Slade Walters and of his surprise when it turned out not to be Slade. He pointed to the cottonwood tree that had knocked the plane from the sky.

The fed made note of all this on his clipboard. "Now then, Mr. Cox, what do you recall about the plane itself? Did you notice anything unusual about how it was flying?"

Gabby thought a moment. "Too low."

The fed didn't bother writing this down. "Just describe the flight path, Mr. Cox. In your own words, please."

Gabby thought again. "Well, I didn't see 'em the first time because I was in the barn. The second time he came in over the grove about there." Gabby pointed to the spot. "Then I waved my arms." Gabby demonstrated. "Then he sorta waggled his wings." Gabby extended his arms and waggled.

The fed had been busily writing, and now he looked up. "Was it your impression that he waggled in response to your waving? That he waggled at you?"

Gabby shrugged, then nodded.

"Anything else, Mr. Cox? Anything that stands out in your mind, even if you think it's not important?"

Gabby shrugged again.

"Anything at all?" the fed pressed.

"Well…long blond hair."

"What about long blond hair?"

"That's what I saw. After the second time. The plane climbed and turned and I saw long blond hair."

To Gabby's surprise, the fed noted this and asked, "Which side of the plane were you looking at when you saw the long blond hair?"

Gabby closed his eyes and thought. "The left."

The fed nodded and noted. "That would've been the pilot."

Sam Stack spoke. "That fit with what you know?"

The fed eyed the sheriff for a moment, and then uncharacteristically answered the question. "Based on our current information, it would fit either the pilot or the passenger."

Sam shrugged. "Well, don't look to me for corroboration. By the time I got close enough to look most of the hair was burnt."

The fed looked sharply at the sheriff. "You entered the crash scene before we got here?"

"Of course. Had to make sure there weren't any survivors."

The fed shook his head and made a note. "Did you remove anything?"

"Of course not."

"Did you touch anything?"

"No," Sam bristled. "This is an accident scene. I know how to treat an accident scene."

The fed looked skeptical. "So you were the first to reach the aircraft after the crash?"

"Yep. Soon as they got the fire out."

"Describe in detail what you saw."

"Two Caucasians, a male and a female, both dead."

"And?"

"And they appeared to have been flying naked."

The fed noted this as if he were recording eye color, not nudity. "Anything else, Sheriff?"

"Possible alcohol use."

The fed looked up. "Based on what?"

"Based on the empty gin bottle lying on the cabin floor."

"Let's not jump to conclusions, Sheriff. That's what autopsies are for."

A hint of a smile played at the corners of Sam Stack's mouth. "Of course."

"Did you note anything else, Sheriff?"

Sam shrugged. "Based on their positions in the cockpit, I'd say he had the controls." A hint of smile again. "And she had his joystick."

The fed's eyes narrowed. "This is a federal investigation, Sheriff. Let's be professional here."

Sam nodded, his smile widening.

The fed eyed Sam for a long moment. "Actually, Sheriff, we're going to need your help with site security."

"I understand."

"No, I'm not sure you do, Sheriff." The fed paused to consider his clipboard. "You see, this appears to be, um, a high-profile crash."

"Meaning?"

"Meaning that the victims are, er, were…celebrities."

"Who?" asked Sam.

The fed paused once more. "Of course, there hasn't been a positive identification of the bodies yet."

"Of course." Sam nodded.

"But based on the flight plan filed in Minneapolis, it appears that the owner of the aircraft was the pilot."

"And he was?"

Another pause. "Sphinx."

Sam let out a low whistle.

"Who?" asked Gabby.

"Sphinx, Gabby. A rock star." Sam turned to the fed. "In fact, didn't he have a concert in Minneapolis last night?"

The fed nodded, but Gabby shook his head in confusion. "Sphinx? That his first name or his last name?"

"His only name," said Sam. "That's all you need if you're a famous rock star."

After all that had happened that day, Gabby was almost afraid to ask the next question, but after a moment he did. "Who was the lady, then?"

"Once again, we don't have positive ID on the bodies yet," the fed said.

"We understand that," said Sam. "Who do you believe the woman to be?"

The fed hesitated. "Sparkle."

"Aw, Jesus," said Sam.

"Who?" asked Gabby.

"Sparkle," the fed repeated.

"Just one name again?"

The fed nodded.

"She another rock star?"

The fed shook is head. "More like a wannabe."

"Well, what's she famous for then?" asked Gabby.

"For being famous, I guess," the fed said with a shrug. Then he turned to Sam. "And that, Sheriff, is why we're going to need a lot of security out here. There's going to be a crowd. And it won't be just the media. You can bet there'll be fans too, plenty of 'em, so line up all the bodies you can find."

Sam nodded grimly.

"And I don't want anyone talking to the media. Everything has to come from NTSB. This thing is going to be enough of a circus without adding a lot of rumors and inaccuracies on top of it."

Sam nodded again.

"And that goes for you too, Mr. Cox. You're not to speak with anyone about this until we issue our final report."

A wave of anxiety swept over Gabby, but its cause wasn't the fed's newest order. The prospect of not talking to people didn't trouble him in the least. But the prospect of the world coming to his farm did.

CHAPTER 3

▼

Gwen Todd sipped white wine as she watched the evening news on TV. It was something she did most nights, and she'd long since gotten past any stigma connected with drinking alone. She lived alone, after all, and she refused to let that deny her the enjoyment of a glass of wine—and some nights she had more than one. This was looking like one of those nights.

Like everyone else in Hayesboro, her attention had been riveted all day by events unfolding just six miles away on the Cox farm. Now as she watched the TV news account, that focus suddenly felt intrusive. Television was supposed to bring the world benignly into your living room, but when it exposed familiar places, places like your own backyard, it was no longer benign.

And in a sense, the Cox farm was Gwen's backyard. She'd grown up on a farm just a mile away, so the Coxes had been neighbors. She was two years younger than Gabby, and for years they rode the same school bus, though they weren't really friends. Friendship would come later, but back then, Gabby rarely spoke to anyone, much less to a girl. In fact, he passed through Hayesboro High largely unnoticed. He didn't compete in athletics or participate in any other extracurricular activity. He was an average student who showed up each day and quietly did his work; then he rode the bus back to the farm and the refuge of chores. No one expected Gabby Cox to distinguish himself. Everyone expected him to live out his days unremarkably on the family farm. So far everyone had been right.

Gwen Todd was different. All through high school she had been Miss Everything. She sang solos in the choir and played clarinet in the band. She starred in stage productions and captained the cheerleading squad. She graduated valedictorian of her class. Unlike Gabby, the townsfolk did have expectations for Gwen, expectations that might've been even greater were she beautiful, but at 5'2" she qualified only as cute. "Cute" had also described the way a ready smile would transform her regular features, but now at age thirty-eight, "cute" had given way to "pleasant," and streaks of gray had begun appearing in her light brown hair. Her smile was still ready, but expectations for her future had faded and she'd become something of a local mystery. Where everyone had been pretty much right about Gabby Cox, most had been wrong about Gwen Todd.

She had started off well enough. After high school she went to the University of Minnesota, where she continued her academic excellence, earning degrees in both music and English. Then it was off to Los Angeles, two time zones behind Minnesota, but years ahead in trend zones. The townsfolk were realistic; they didn't expect "cute" Gwen to become a movie star, but they did expect to read about her in the papers or see her on TV before long. Surely there was a place in California for Hayesboro's best.

She came home after one year. There were no rumors of scandal or unrequited love. There were no tales of Tinsel Town disillusionment. She simply came home, and to everyone's surprise, she never left again. She took a job at the Hayesboro Public Library, and after five years she became the head librarian. For a time she lived with her parents on the farm, then she bought a small house in town where in the summer she could sit on her front porch and enjoy concerts in the band shell across the street in the park. In addition to her library duties, she directed stage and musical productions at the high school. She soloed in the community choir. She delighted people in ways they had always known she would. She just wasn't doing it in California to the greater glory of Hayesboro, and that, coupled with the fact the she never spoke of her time out west, cloaked her with an aura of mystery, at least to the extent that a librarian can be mysterious.

Gabby Cox was a regular patron of the library. Apart from his farm, reading seemed his only interest, and over the years his visits to the library led to friendship with Gwen Todd. Of course, it wasn't a chatty friendship—he didn't say much—but she came to know him by what he read. Mostly he preferred biographies, especially biographies of U.S. presidents, and among those, Lincoln and Teddy Roosevelt were his favorites. She had tried to interest him in fiction a time or two, but he always declined.

"Thing about fiction," he once said, "is you can never tell what's the truth and what's not."

"You can find as much truth in fiction an you can in nonfiction," she countered. "Besides, just because something's nonfiction doesn't mean it's true."

Gabby was shocked at the idea that someone might write untruths about Abraham Lincoln. It was a concept he couldn't grasp.

"What about poetry?" she then suggested. Gwen wrote some poetry herself.

Gabby declined again. "I can never figure out what they're trying to say."

"Truth isn't always black and white," she said. "Sometimes you only find it in the nuances."

Nuances, especially poetic ones, were beyond Gabby's grasp too, so he stayed with his presidents and that version of the truth, and now as Gwen sipped her second glass of wine, she felt a wave of sympathy for her quiet friend. She knew the attention, the invasion of his privacy, would be painful. She also feared that Gabby had only an inkling of what was to come. Gwen had more than an inkling. She'd once stood close to the crash of a pop idol herself, a crash that left her soul scarred. Yes, she understood what was coming at Gabby, but she could only say so much to warn him. To say more would mean speaking of things she'd vowed to never speak of again.

CHAPTER 4

▼

The TV news account of Sphinx's and Sparkle's deaths that Gwen Todd
watched had included aerial views shot from a helicopter and also ground
close-ups shot by a mobile unit that had arrived late in the afternoon. The
close proximity of the mobile unit, however, failed to reap much in the
way of detail. A reporter shoved a mike in the face of Howard Blake, head
of the National Transportation Safety Board team that was investigating
the crash. Blake glared and reported that he would have nothing to report
until their investigation was complete. The camera and mike were then
turned on Sheriff Sam Stack, who stared impassively from behind aviator
sunglasses when the reporter asked if crashes of this sort happened often in
his county.

"No," said Sam after a long moment.

"Do you have any idea what caused the crash?"

"No," said Sam.

"Were there any indications, any radio transmissions, that the plane was
in trouble?"

"No," said Sam.

"Can you tell us anything about the condition of the bodies?"

Sam hesitated an instant. "No."

"This is a bit more than you usually deal with, Sheriff. Are your people
up to it?"

"Yes," said Sam.

"Were you a Sphinx fan, Sheriff?"

The question seemed to startle Sam, then he answered, "No."

The reporter turned and sliced his hand across his throat, signaling the cameraman to stop taping, and turned back to Sam. "Look, Sheriff, this is a big story, bigger than just the local news. The network'll pick it up, of course, and since we're a CNN affiliate, they'll be running it too. The whole goddamn country's gonna see it, so how about something more than just yes and no?"

Sam nodded toward the barn. "Blake's in charge. Talk to him."

"It'll be a week before that asshole says a thing, and then it'll just be a bunch of technical crap. I need something now, and I need details. The country wants the gore, Sheriff!"

Sam shook his head. "No comment."

"Now wait a minute, Sheriff, what about the property owner?" The reporter glanced at his notepad. "What about this Cox guy? Did he witness the crash?"

"No comment."

"Look, just get him to come out and talk to me. It's his big chance to get his mug on national TV."

"Mr. Cox has also declined comment. He has a right to privacy, you know."

"Bullshit! A fucking rock star crashed into his goddamn barn, Sheriff. He doesn't have a right to shit anymore."

Sam shook his head and walked away.

With no eyewitness to speak of gruesome gore to the camera, the reporter was forced to fall back on his own imagination and eloquence. He positioned himself in front of the charred ruins of the barn and then faced the camera. "In a few hours the sun will set over this normally bucolic scene, but today the farm of Mr. Gabriel Cox has been anything but peaceful. It has, in fact, been a place of great tragedy, a tragedy that now holds the world's rapt attention as millions of fans mourn the sudden passing of rock 'n' roll giant, Sphinx, and the darling of American pop culture, Sparkle. At times such as this, we take heart in knowing that, though the sun will soon set, it will also surely rise tomorrow. But that optimism will be small solace to those many fans burdened with the knowledge that these two bright lights will never shine again.

"There are many questions, all unanswered. What caused Sphinx's plane to crash? And why here of all places? Was it destiny? Is there some fateful connection between this simple farm and the superstar, a place and person now inextricably bound for all time? Are there clues to be found in Sphinx's music? Or do the answers lie beyond the stars?" The reporter paused and looked knowingly at the camera. "Only time will tell."

* * * *

The other news crews fared no better at finding the gore that their viewers demanded, and Gabby watched with relief from inside the house as the last mobile unit headed out of his driveway at eight in the evening. Sam Stack had posted a patrol car and two deputies out at the end of the driveway, and from that point they had controlled access into the yard. The media had to be let in, of course, but the feds and two more of Sam's deputies kept them at least a hundred feet from the actual crash site. Now they were gone, but Gabby's relief didn't last for long.

At eight thirty, Gabby came out of the house and sat on the porch steps with a bottle of beer. It was still hot and the beer was cold and it calmed his nerves. Fifteen minutes later Sam Stack trudged up the walk, removed his ball cap, and wiped sweat from his brow before putting his cap back on.

"Hot one, huh, Sam?"

Sam nodded.

"Want a beer?"

"I'd love one, but I'm still on duty." Sam sat on the step next to Gabby, then removed his sunglasses and slipped them into his shirt pocket. "Aw, what the fuck. Yeah, get me a beer. After a day like this, no one can bitch about one lousy beer."

Gabby went into the house and came back in a minute with a beer for Sam and another for himself. They sipped in silence and watched the feds comb through the wreckage. The sun had just set, and the feds had rigged spotlights so that they could keep working; and the bright lights made the charred ruins seem all the more surreal.

"Sure hope them fellas get outta here pretty soon," said Gabby.

Sam nodded. "Me too. This is raising hell with my overtime budget."

They lapsed into silence again, and after a minute, Gabby pointed out toward the road. "Now what?"

Sam turned his head. Out across the cornfield dust billowed up against the red evening sky all along the county road that led from the highway. It was as if a great herd was stampeding, and the stampede appeared headed for the Cox farm. Before Sam could say anything, the radio mike hanging from his shoulder crackled, and a moment later a voice said, "Come in, Sheriff."

It was one of the deputies posted out at the end of the driveway, and Sam keyed the mike. "Yeah, Al, what's up?"

"Bunch of cars coming."

"More media?"

"Don't think so. Looks like regular cars. All different kinds and lots of 'em. Couple buses too."

"Aw, shit," Sam muttered to himself, then he keyed the mike. "Well, keep 'em out there, Al. Nobody gets into the yard."

"Who are they?" asked Gabby.

Sam ignored him and keyed the mike again. "Dispatch?"

Dispatch responded in a second and Sam issued terse orders. "Get everybody available out here and quick. We're gonna need a lot more crowd control. And get on the Hayesboro police too. This is looking like a mutual aid situation. I need at least a dozen officers altogether."

Gabby listened with growing alarm. "Who are they, Sam? Who's coming?"

Sam shook his head. "I was afraid of this. I was hoping the feds would finish up and get the wreckage outta here so there wouldn't be much to attract them, but it looks like they found us."

"Who, Sam? Who found us?"

Sam tilted his bottle up, gulped the last of his beer, and stood up. "Fans, Gabby. Sphinx and Sparkle's fans found us."

*   *   *   *

They came by the hundreds, then by the thousands, in the last light of day. There was a great confusion of dust and honking out on the county road, and Sam sent the two deputies from the yard out to help. Five minutes later, Deputy Al radioed back a report.

"Road's solid with cars for at least a half mile. The reinforcements from town couldn't get through. They radioed that they're going around the long way. Be another ten minutes at least."

Sam keyed his mike. "I heard 'em, Al. Can you handle things till they get here?"

"For now. Nobody's tried to get past yet, but there's a helluva lot of 'em." There was a pause and then, "Aw, shit, some of 'em are heading into the corn."

"Stop 'em," said Sam.

"How? The field runs a good quarter mile along the road. There're thousands of them and four of us. How the hell we supposed to stop 'em? Shoot 'em?"

"Don't even think about it. And send those other two back in. Looks like we're gonna need 'em more here than out there."

Sam was standing in the yard next to his car and now Gabby joined him. "What's going on, Sam?"

"They're coming through the corn."

Gabby's eyes grew wide. "Shit, Sam, that's trespassing. They can't do that."

"Well, we haven't figured out how to stop 'em just yet."

"Shoot 'em! Hell, they're breaking the law."

"Gabby..." Sam started to say more but then just shook his head.

The two deputies came in from the road, and Sam posted them along the fifty yards where the cornfield bordered the yard. They could hear shouts and the rustle of people running through the corn, and the sounds grew louder and louder.

"I'll get my shotgun and help," said Gabby.

Sam whirled and jabbed a finger at Gabby. "You get in the house, Gabby, and stay there. And so help me God, if I see you out here with a shotgun, I'll shoot you myself."

"Goddamn it, Sam, this is my property."

"I don't care. This is my show. Now get in the goddamn house!"

The first person out of the cornfield was a teenage girl. She broke into the yard between the two deputies, and Sam ran to cut her off. She wore tight jeans and a tighter top and her face was streaked with tears and sweat and she clutched a bouquet of flowers against small bouncing breasts. She stopped for a moment, looked at Sam and the deputies, then she wailed, "Sphinx!" and took off again.

Sam caught up with her and grabbed her arm. She whirled and swung the bouquet at his head. He ducked and caught her other arm. "Just hold on, miss!"

"Sphinx!" she wailed again.

"You're trespassing on private property, miss!" This came from Gabby, who hadn't gone to the house as ordered.

Three more broke from the corn: two girls and a boy. The deputies corralled the girls, but the boy managed to slip by and sprint for the barn.

"You can't go there," Gabby called after him.

Now they were pouring out of the corn, all sizes and shapes. Mostly they were quite young, teenagers, but some were older, aging rock 'n' roll groupies. Many carried flowers. Sam and Gabby and the deputies tried to stop them, but they could only grab a few and the rest flew by, making a beeline for the charred ruin with an airplane rudder sticking up from its midst.

Howard Blake ran up. "Sheriff, they're contaminating the crash scene. Do something!"

Sam gave him a weary look. "We're doing everything we can."

"Well, do more! Washington's not going to like this, and it's your failure, Sheriff, not mine. I'll make that clear in my report."

Sam looked toward the barn, where people now ran in every direction, picking up bits of wreckage and even the small blue flags that the feds had used to mark them. A teenage boy raced from the barn with a propeller blade cradled in his arms. Two feds chased close behind. Sam shook his head and keyed the mike hanging from his shoulder. It would be the first time in his long law enforcement career that he had to call out the National Guard.

*   *   *   *

The additional deputies and the Hayesboro police officers arrived five minutes later. They were only ten altogether, no match for the crowd, but together with the feds and deputies already there, they did manage to secure a perimeter around the crash site. Frenzied fans continued pouring out of the corn, and they massed around the perimeter. Bouquets of flowers sailed through the air as they were heaved over the perimeter into the ruins. Some started to sing, and soon they all were singing. The music was strange to Gabby's ear, and the mob choir's words were indistinguishable, but everyone seemed to know them.

The National Guard unit from Hayesboro got there just before midnight, and only then were they able to bring the crowd under control. Fans trudged by the hundred back out the driveway, but many more ran back into the corn with elements of the Guard and deputies in pursuit. Their earlier path through the corn had been a direct one, and they had stomped down most of the stalks in a ten-acre triangle. Now they swung wider, trampling new areas, and it was two in the morning before the Guard declared the field cleared of fans, though in the darkness no one could be sure. It was four in the morning before most of the cars were cleared from the road leading to the Cox farm, a task complicated by new arrivals streaming in. The Guard set up a roadblock a mile away where the county road intersected the highway, but determined fans simply drove through neighboring fields, causing extensive crop damage.

First light came just after five and with it an uneasy calm. Some of the Guard and deputies stayed on to man the perimeter and roadblocks, and everyone else retired from the scene. At five thirty, Gabby stood by himself in his yard, looking out upon, by his estimate, twenty acres of trampled corn. He shook his head. It was amazing that no one had been seriously hurt, and for that he was grateful. He regretted his earlier outburst. He knew that you don't shoot people for simple trespass. He was thankful that Sam Stack had kept a calm head because for a brief moment the mob had transformed Gabby into something that now frightened him. His gaze shifted from the trampled corn to the burnt barn, and he shook his head again. In one day he'd lost a good barn and twelve pigs and twenty acres of corn. Two people had died as well, and of course he regretted that, but he regretted something else just as much: a lost sense of safe harbor in his own home. It'd been one hell of a day.

CHAPTER 5

▼

Gwen Todd slowed her Toyota as she neared the Cox farm. It had been two days since the crash, and apart from the charred ruins of the barn, things looked more or less normal. The feds had loaded the wrecked plane on a truck and moved to phase 2 in their investigation, which would take place in a hanger at the Minneapolis-St. Paul International Airport. With the plane gone, the fans had left too, and with them the Guard and Sam Stack's deputies, and seeing the empty yard, Gwen almost turned in at Gabby's drive. She had thought of him often over the past two days; she'd hoped that he might drop by the library so that they could talk, but she wasn't surprised that he hadn't. He was probably sick of having people around, and that was why she didn't stop, why she drove on to her original destination.

The Todd farm was a mile further on from the Cox place. She turned in at the drive and parked in the graveled yard near the red brick house that had been home for much of her life. She climbed from the car and walked to the back door, and there she paused. Since her mother's death two years earlier, Gwen made this trip each day, and each day she paused at the door, wondering what she would find inside.

She never found L. R. Todd in a cheerful mood anymore. Those days had ended with her mother, and now Gwen was happy if her father was just reasonably alert. Too often lately she hadn't found even that. He no longer shaved every day, nor did he shower as regularly as he should, and though Gwen kept up with his laundry, L. R. often went several days between clean clothes. Some days she found him sitting at the kitchen table in his underwear, staring dully at nothing in particular. One day she found him standing naked by the refrigerator, a cold pork chop in his hand, and he didn't bother to cover himself when she walked in. That frightened her. It made her seriously doubt whether her father was still capable of living alone. She talked to his doctor and to the manager of the assisted living facility in Hayesboro, and she considered intervening; then she talked to her father.

Just the thought of leaving the farm had worked a remarkable change. L. R. had been born on the farm, it was the only place he'd ever lived, so the prospect of living elsewhere produced a sudden improvement in his personal hygiene, if not his mood. For a time he shaved and showered and put on clean clothes each morning. He began eating better. Gwen had hoped it would last, but over the past few weeks he had started slipping again, and she feared that one day soon she would have to consider intervention once more. Either that, or one day, she would pause to wonder at the back door and then walk inside the house to find him dead.

Now she took a breath and opened the door. L. R. Todd was fully clothed and clean-shaven and sipping coffee over a newspaper at the kitchen table. His eyes were brighter than they'd been in days. He was energized by evil.

As she walked in, he looked up from the paper and exclaimed, "A hundred and fifty acres!"

"What're you talking about, Dad?"

"The crops those goddamn city folks ran down. A hundred and fifty acres! Says so right here in the paper. And what'd anybody do about it? Nothing! The law just mollycoddles criminals these days. Man's got no right to protect his property anymore."

Gwen was always glad to find her father alert, but she wasn't sure that this day's mental acuity was a good thing. "Well, Gabriel lost a bunch of those acres—and his barn too."

L.R.'s hair was still jet black, despite his seventy-eight years, and his bushy eyebrows were just as black, and they knitted now in a moment of confusion. "The city folks ran down Gabby's barn too?"

"No, Dad, an airplane crashed into it. Remember, you saw it on the news. We talked about it yesterday."

His eyebrows knitted again. "An airplane? Weren't Slade Walters?"

"No, Dad, it was that singer, remember? A singer and his girlfriend."

L. R. thought a moment, then he nodded slowly. "City folks in an airplane?"

"Well...yeah."

"Goddamn city folks!" L. R. shook his head. "They got no respect for the countryside."

L. R. Todd had always divided good and evil with the same line that separated country folks and city folks, an arbitrary division he used more readily now as his understanding of events grew more vague. Gwen tried to change the subject. "Well, it's all over now, Dad. All the city people've left and things are getting back to normal."

"Normal?" L. R. snorted. "Don't you believe it. My sweet corn's getting ripe, so they'll be back. It's the same every year."

L. R. hadn't farmed his land in ten years. He rented the tillable acres out, but each year the renter planted an acre of sweet corn for him next to the grove. The sweet corn patch had three different varieties so that it didn't all ripen at the same time, and it was just enough to make L. R. feel as if he were still a farmer. He took joy in sharing the corn with his neighbors, or anyone else who stopped by and asked permission to pick a dozen ears. Pilfering wasn't a problem because the patch was well removed from the road, but that didn't stop L. R. from turning reports of pilfering in nearby sweet corn fields grown for the cannery in Hayesboro into stories of his own. And most of that pilfering was done by locals, not people from the big city, but when it came to good and evil, L. R. usually had Hayesboro folks on the same side of the line as Minneapolis folks. It was a subject that Gwen wasn't going to get into this day and she stood to leave.

"Maybe I'll pick a few ears for my supper," she said.

"Help yourself. It's the twelve rows closest to the grove. Next stuff's a good week away."

"Maybe I'll pick a few extra ears and drop them off for Gabriel."

L. R. nodded. "Good idea. Least we can do for a man what got his barn wrecked by city folks."

CHAPTER 6

▼

Gabby had his John Deere tractor pulled up to the charred barn, and he was tossing wilted flowers into the loader when the car drove into the yard. An insurance adjuster had finally come by earlier that morning, and he'd assured Gabby that Sphinx's insurance would cover everything, even the cleanup, but the wilted bouquets had begun smelling like death in the hot sun so Gabby had decided to clean them up himself.

The car was a Cadillac, and Gabby guessed it to be about ten years old. He kept tossing flowers into the loader, hoping that whoever it was would go away. He didn't want to talk to anyone. He'd talked to enough people in the past two days to satisfy his conversational needs for a year, but then the Cadillac's horn sounded a long, impatient honk, and Gabby sighed. He really didn't want to talk to anyone, but he'd been taught at an early age that strangers driving into the yard were entitled to good manners.

As Gabby walked toward the Cadillac, he noticed rust showing on the rear fenders, and he revised his estimate of the car's age to fifteen years. A man climbed from the car. He was balding with heavy jowls. He wore a bow tie and wide suspenders, and as he walked to meet Gabby he tried to button his suit coat, but his belly wouldn't allow it so he let the coat hang open.

"H. Landon Beard," the man barked, thrusting his right hand out to pump Gabby's while holding out a business card in his left hand. "Mr. Cox, I presume."

Gabby nodded and looked at the card. H. Landon Beard was an attorney-at-law, and Gabby felt a twinge of anxiety. In addition to manners, he'd also learned at an early age that a lawyer driving unannounced into the yard was seldom a good thing.

As if sensing Gabby's anxiety, H. Landon offered a disarming smile. "This is your lucky day, Mr. Cox, because I'm here to offer you my services."

Gabby studied the card again. H. Landon specialized in personal injury. "Don't reckon I need a lawyer."

H. Landon gave a hearty laugh. "Oh, Mr. Cox, Mr. Cox, you do indeed need a lawyer. And in fact you need me."

Gabby kept studying the card because it allowed him to avoid eye contact. H. Landon was from Minneapolis. "I don't do much lawyering, and when I do, John Kirk in Hayesboro takes care of it."

H. Landon laughed again. "No, no, no, Mr. Cox, your situation goes way beyond what some country lawyer can handle." He paused and rested a meaty hand on Gabby's shoulder and then lowered his voice. "You're going up against the big boys from the insurance companies, Mr. Cox. You need a specialist."

"Well…a fella from the insurance company was here earlier, and he said everything'd get taken care of and not to worry."

H. Landon continued to find humor in everything Gabby said, and now he laughed even harder. "Mr. Cox, those insurance boys'll eat you for breakfast, lunch and dinner unless you get the right kind of representation. And Mr. Cox, I am the right kind of representation. You need a personal injury specialist like me."

"But I ain't injured."

H. Landon chuckled and shook his head. "Believe me, Mr. Cox, you are injured. You are so very injured. The first law in these things, you see, is that the injury is proportional to the depth of the injurer's pockets."

Gabby wasn't sure what that meant. "Still don't see that I'm injured."

H. Landon thrust his hand at the barn. "Behold your injury, Mr. Cox." H. Landon swung around and pointed to trampled corn. "You are surrounded by injury."

Gabby had to nod. His barn and his cornfield had been injured. There was no denying that.

"And that's just the beginning," said H. Landon. "How are you feeling, Mr. Cox?"

"Pretty good, I reckon."

"No, Mr. Cox, how are you really feeling? Are you anxious? Having trouble sleeping? Not much appetite?"

Gabby shrugged and then nodded.

"Mental anguish!" thundered H. Landon. "I can see the suffering in your eyes. You are a victim, Mr. Cox." H. Landon draped a consoling arm around Gabby's shoulders and lowered his voice. "May I call you Gabriel?"

Gabby nodded.

"Gabriel, did you have livestock in that barn?"

"Twelve pigs."

"Now dead?"

Gabby nodded. "Rendering plant came and hauled 'em away yesterday."

"Were you close to those pigs, Gabriel?"

For the first time, Gabby made eye contact with the lawyer. "They were pigs."

"Well, did they have names?"

Gabby took a step back and repeated, "They were pigs."

H. Landon studied Gabby's face for a moment. "Just bacon, huh?"

Gabby nodded.

"Well, that's not a problem, Gabriel. There's still more than enough injury here. Hell, your mental anguish alone'll be worth a couple million. Then there's the barn. I expect that'd been around a while."

Gabby nodded.

"I expect you had quite a sentimental attachment to that barn."

No nod at this. Instead, Gabby eyed the lawyer for a moment. "Look, Mr. Beard, if I need to do some lawyering, I'm sure John Kirk can handle it, so if you don't mind—"

H. Landon grabbed Gabby's arm. "Don't decide now, Gabriel. At least sleep on it. There's a lot at stake here, so don't rush to judgment. Just sleep on it and I'll get back to you tomorrow."

Gabby didn't want to see H. Landon the next day or any other day, and he was about to abandon his manners when another car drove into the yard. It was Gwen Todd's Toyota.

"That the missus?" asked H. Landon.

"No." Gabby shook his head. "But you oughta leave now, Mr. Beard."

H. Landon raised his eyebrows. "Got a little something going here? A nooner maybe?"

Once more, Gabby wasn't sure what the lawyer meant, but he didn't like the tone. "Look, Mr.—"

"Just say you'll sleep on it, and I'm outta here. The bottom line, Gabriel, is that you've been injured, so someone's gotta pay, and I can get you a good payday. Just sleep on it."

"Okay, I'll sleep on it," said Gabby, just to be rid of the man.

H. Landon paused by his car as Gwen climbed from hers with a paper sack. He looked her up and down and grinned. "Good day, ma'am."

Gwen watched as H. Landon drove from the yard, spinning gravel, then she turned to Gabby. "Hope I didn't interrupt anything."

"Nah. He's just some lawyer looking for business."

She watched the Cadillac disappear down the road. "He probably won't be the last."

That hadn't occurred to Gabby, and the thought of a procession of H. Landons sent a shiver down his spine.

Gwen held out her sack. "I brought you some sweet corn. It's from Dad's patch by the grove."

"Thanks." Gabby took the sack, and they made brief eye contact before he cast his eyes awkwardly to the ground. "I'll cook it up for my supper," he added without looking up.

Another awkward moment passed before Gwen said, "Well, I'll be going. I was just out checking on Dad, and since his corn was ripe I thought you might…"

He looked up. "You don't have to go."

"But you're busy."

"Nothing that won't wait." Gabby still felt clumsy standing with her there in the yard, but suddenly he didn't want her to leave. "Would you like some lemonade?"

"Um…sure. Lemonade would be nice, Gabriel."

Gabby seated her in one of the two rocking chairs on the porch and went into the kitchen. He was glad she'd come, glad she was staying, but he couldn't get over his sense of awkwardness. He always enjoyed their visits at the library. Were it not for those visits, were it not for Gwen, he probably wouldn't read as much as he did. His talks with Gwen were an inseparable part of his reading habit, and he also liked that she called him Gabriel. She was the only one in town who did, and it seemed to return the respect he felt for her. And it wasn't just that she used his real name; when H. Landon had called him Gabriel, it hadn't felt respectful at all. He took two glasses from the cupboard and added ice, then lemonade from the pitcher he kept in the refrigerator. Yes, his friendship with Gwen was rooted in respect, and it was also rooted in the library—that was really the only place they ever saw each other—and the library was hushed and respectful, never awkward. Now, here on his farm, the place where he was rooted, it felt awkward to be with her. He didn't understand that, but he was still glad she was there.

Out on the porch, he handed her a glass and sat down in the other rocking chair. The rockers had belonged to his parents and before that to his grandparents, and sitting in them now with Gwen helped ease his awkwardness a bit.

She sipped her lemonade. "Delicious, Gabriel. Do you squeeze your own lemons?"

"It's from powder." Gabby always chose convenience in the kitchen. He was a bachelor, after all.

They sipped in silence for a time, then Gwen said, "This has been a terrible thing. How are you holding up?"

Gabby shrugged.

"I know how you value your privacy, so it must've been awful with all those people running wild out here."

He shrugged again. "Better now." He looked at her, and she smiled, and he looked down at his lemonade. It was the same smile she gave him in the library, and there he always returned it, but here on his porch, it was different somehow. Then something else happened that was different. He had an urge to talk. Suddenly, the emotions of the past two days began forming words on his tongue.

"You wanna know what bothers me most about all this?"

She nodded.

"It ain't the barn or the pigs or the corn or any of that. All that stuff can be replaced, and so can my privacy. Two people got killed, and they can't be replaced, and that bothers me plenty, but there's something else that bothers me just as much."

Gwen rocked and sipped and waited.

"Why here? That's what I can't figure out. Why'd it have to happen on my farm?"

"It was an accident, Gabriel. Accidents happen where they happen. It's by chance."

Gabby shook his head. "That's the part that bothers me. I don't think it was chance at all. I can't shake the feeling that this Sphinx fella came looking for me, that he meant all this to happen—and meant it to happen here."

"That's human nature, Gabriel. We personalize things. We see ourselves connected to things that have nothing to do with us. I'm sure the federal investigation'll make all that clear."

In his mind Gabby saw the plane dive again and again; he saw wings waggle; he glimpsed long blonde hair. No, he wished he wasn't a part of it, that it was pure chance, but something kept telling him that it wasn't so, that indeed he was a part of it.

Something else bothered him too, something that seemed somehow related to everything else, and now it simply leaped from his tongue: "They were naked."

Gwen's eyes grew wide. "Sphinx and Sparkle?"

Gabby felt his face turn crimson, and he silently cursed his mutinous tongue.

"Did…did you see them?" she asked.

He shook his head. "Sam Stack told me. And I don't think I was supposed to tell you, not till the investigation's done."

"Don't worry. I won't say a word." She thought a moment. "Do you know anything about Sphinx? Or Sparkle for that matter?"

Gabby shook his head. "Never heard of 'em till now. And I wish I never had."

"That might be part of the problem. They were so different from anything you could imagine, and if you understood what bizarre people they were, then this might not seem so…bizarre. It might help you put it in perspective."

Gabby shrugged and said nothing. He was determined to keep his tongue in check.

"Stop by the library tomorrow, Gabriel. I'll put some information together for you. It might help."

Gabby looked at her, and this time when she smiled, he managed to hold her gaze and return her smile. Then he risked freeing his tongue to utter, "Thanks. And thanks for the corn."

CHAPTER 7

▼

After college, when Gwen Todd moved to L.A., she had no job lined up, only the confidence that she'd find one and a desire to be where the action was. For the first month, the action was in a cheap motel off Sunset Boulevard, and on more than one occasion, she almost packed up and went home, but then she found a job, and after that, she found an apartment. The apartment was in Venice, just a block off the beach and a short walk from Marina Del Rey. She couldn't afford it—the rent took over half her salary—but "affording" was a Minnesota thing, and she was a California girl now, and Venice seemed like where a California girl ought to live.

The Chrome Agency ranked with Hollywood's elite. Like other agencies in the entertainment industry, it negotiated contracts and handled public relations, but those were only the obvious functions. Chrome did much more. At Chrome the client surrendered control of his or her life; clients submitted themselves to molding and reshaping and mothering, and they did it willingly because the Chrome label opened doors. Chrome was a small agency, just a handful of associates in addition to its namesake founder, and there were never more than six or so clients at a time.

"Some of these agencies out here think you gotta represent a huge stable of talent to make a buck," Ron Chrome had explained to Gwen on the day he hired her as an associate. "They're wrong. In fact, I don't represent talent. Talent's a dime a dozen out here. It's a commodity. The real money's in superstars, and just having talent won't make 'em a super star, not by a long shot. For that they need me. That's what I do. I make superstars. Nothing more, nothing less."

They were seated in Chrome's office, and Gwen marveled at the array of celebrities pictured on the paneled walls.

"That impress you?" Chrome asked.

Gwen nodded.

"Like to see your picture up there someday?"

Gwen shrugged and smiled.

"Ain't gonna happen."

Gwen's smile faded.

"Lemme tell you why I hired you, Toddy." Ron Chrome never called his associates by their given names. "One, I hired you because you're from the Midwest. I like that. Good work ethic. These West Coast kids are all screwed up by the time they're fifteen. Two, I hired you because you're smart. What's the point in hiring dummies? And three, I hired you because you've got talent, in some cases more than the egos you'll be working with, but that talent ain't gonna put your picture on my wall. What it's gonna do is help you understand and deal with the bastards, and believe me, you'll need it because they can be a real pain in the ass."

Gwen managed a wry smile. "So I'm talented, maybe more talented than some stars, but still not star material?"

Chrome leaned forward and thrust out his jaw. He was a small man with dark intense eyes that sparked with energy. "You been listening to me, Toddy? Talent's got nothing to do with it. If all they needed was talent, then they wouldn't need us. But they do need us because we know how to turn 'em into stars. Right?"

Gwen smiled and nodded, not trusting any words she might utter at that moment.

"It's business, Toddy. Never forget that. It's just business, and the stars are our product. And in the long run, you're way better off on the business side. Oh, I know you came out here to work in front of a camera—everybody does—but you're better off on the business side. You'll keep your sanity a helluva lot longer."

Tess Snow was twenty-two years old, the same age as Gwen. She'd had her first country hit at eighteen, and now she had a net worth approaching twenty million dollars. She was a natural blonde with a pretty face and a good body, so it was only a matter of time before Nashville connected with Hollywood. Her music helped launch her into movies, and in turn, movies sold her music to a larger audience, and so on, around and around, up and away. Tess Snow was already a star and on her way to becoming a superstar. Tess Snow was a client of the Chrome Agency.

One of Gwen's first assignments at the agency was to go to Tess's house and escort her to the grand opening of a pricey steakhouse. It was a publicity event conceived by Ron Chrome, and it was scripted to include Tess's "impromptu" rendering of her first hit: "Red Meat," which included the lyric, "I like mine lean with a bone in it."

The opening was scheduled for six in the evening, but Chrome told Gwen to be at Tess's house no later than three.

"Why so early?" Gwen asked.

"So you can make sure she's ready," said Chrome, then adding, "and also that she stays ready. Talk to her. Watch TV with her. Hold her hand, but no booze and no pills."

Gwen got to Tess's house at three sharp, but when she rang the doorbell, there was no answer. She waited and then rang the bell again, and when there was still no answer, she let herself in—the agency had a key to Tess's house, of course. Once inside, Gwen called Tess's name and listened. Silence. Gwen gingerly made her way to the back of the house with the growing fear that she'd blown her assignment, that she'd find Tess befogged by some forbidden substance. She finally found Tess in the master bedroom, where her substance of choice that afternoon was a young Latino named Hector, who subsequently turned out to be her pool boy.

Hector seemed embarrassed when he looked up to see Gwen standing in the doorway, and he jumped from the bed and began pulling on his pants. Tess didn't seem embarrassed in the least. She casually pulled a sheet to her waist but didn't bother covering her breasts as she leaned back against a pile of pillows. "You from the agency?" she asked.

Gwen nodded, too dumbstruck to speak or move.

Tess waved her hand toward Hector who was now pulling on his T-shirt. "Don't mind him. A little slumming helps pass the time, if you know what I mean."

Gwen found her voice. "Um…sure. Whatever."

"Hey, don't look so disapproving. Ron told you no booze or dope, right? He always does. He thinks he's my goddamn mother."

Gwen nodded.

Tess waved at Hector again. "Well, he ain't booze, honey, and he ain't dope either, so you've done your job."

Gwen stepped back to let Hector pass through the doorway as Tess added, "Come a little earlier next time and join us."

*   *   *   *

Gwen sipped white wine and used the remote to change TV channels. She'd been watching the evening news, but if asked, she couldn't have repeated any of it. Her thoughts had been filled with California memories, memories that had haunted her constantly since a rock star crashed into Gabby Cox's barn.

CHAPTER 8

▼

They came in the night.

Normally Buck's barking would have roused Gabby, but Buck had been hit by a truck the month before, and Gabby hadn't gotten around to replacing her yet. Buck had been a black Lab, the fifth in a series of dogs dating to Gabby's childhood, and each had been a black Lab, and each had been named Buck. The most recent Buck was actually a bitch, but by the fifth dog tradition ruled out any other name, and in any event, Buck was dead, so Gabby slept through the night.

At five thirty, he came downstairs in boxer shorts and a T-shirt, as he did each morning. He turned on the coffeemaker that he'd prepared the night before, and as it gurgled and perked, he stood at the kitchen window and scratched his crotch while he evaluated the coming day—another part of his morning routine. The eastern sky glowed a soft shade of coral; the day would start clear. And hot. The sun wasn't yet up, and the large round thermometer hanging on the porch post already read seventy-four degrees. Then Gabby's gaze swung toward the barn. He stopped scratching, and his eyes widened as they fell on the camper parked there.

The camper was white with a single horizontal brown stripe. It was about twenty feet long with a sleeping compartment extending out over the van-like cab, the sort of vehicle Gabby saw on the highway every day, heading to and from Minnesota's lakes. He stared intently for a long moment but detected no movement or activity. He listened too, but heard only the coffeemaker's gurgle, and after a full minute his curiosity demanded a closer inspection. He pulled on a pair of cowboy boots that stood by the door, then he paused and thought of grabbing his shotgun too. It was right there, hanging in its rack on the kitchen wall, but then he remembered his scary emotional response the night the mob had trampled his corn. The shotgun was a bad idea. It was best left on the rack, but hanging just beneath it was a baseball bat—a lesser weapon, but a weapon nonetheless—and Gabby grabbed it instead.

He walked slowly across the yard, taking care to soften the crunch of his boots on the gravel. At twenty feet, he stopped and eyed the camper from end to end. Still no sign of anyone. He listened again, but only a mourning dove's call broke the silence of the calm morning air. He edged toward the cab, stopping two feet from the driver's door, and then leaned forward and peered into the window. Empty. At least, it was empty of people, but the cab was filled with trash, with fast food sacks and discarded aluminum cans.

"Hey, man, what's up?"

Gabby spun around, raising the bat as he did.

The man had come around the back of the camper, and he stood there now, hands on hips and a grin on his face.

"Who the hell are you?" Gabby demanded, inching the bat higher.

"Name's Jack Sand. And you don't need that bat, man. Like, I'm not gonna make any trouble."

Jack Sand looked to be about twenty. He was taller than Gabby, but more slender, and he wore khaki shorts and a T-shirt and sandals. His dark red hair was parted down the middle and hung almost to his shoulders. He looked completely out of place in Gabby's barnyard, but his easy grin dispelled any sense of threat.

Gabby lowered the bat. "What's your business, then?"

Before Jack Sand could answer, a young woman came around the back of the camper. She stopped when she saw Gabby, smiled shyly, and continued on to Jack Sand's side, where she took his arm.

Jack Sand looked at her, his grin widening. "And this is Teal Osborne."

Like Sand, Teal Osborne looked about twenty, was tall and slender, and stood with a straightness that underscored her slenderness. She also wore shorts and a T-shirt and sandals, and her blonde hair was straight and long, falling below her shoulders. Where Jack Sand's grin was confident, her smile was shy.

"So you got a name, man?" asked Jack Sand.

Gabby didn't answer right away. He was the property owner, the one who ought to be asking the questions, and it didn't seem right that he should have to answer one. "Cox," he said finally. "Gabby Cox."

"Nice to meet you Gabby Cox," said Jack Sand.

"I like your outfit," said Teal Osborne.

Only then did it occur to Gabby that he was standing in front of strangers, wearing only boxers, a T-shirt and cowboy boots. He felt his face redden and he raised the baseball bat to cover himself, but realizing that it covered nothing, he lowered it again.

"I happen to be the owner here," he said, "so state your business."

"We just need to be here, man," said Jack Sand. "We've come a long way, and we need to be here; that's all."

"You from Minneapolis?"

"Minneapolis! Hell, that's just down the road. I said a long way. Like, New York, man."

Gabby's eyes widened. To his knowledge, he'd never met anyone from New York. New York was a place he knew only from television.

"From New York City?"

"Um…a little north of there."

Before Gabby could ask how far north, two more people walked out from behind the camper.

"How many people you got in there?" he asked instead.

"Just the four of us," said Jack Sand. "This is Kevin Calm and Meredith Towne."

Kevin Calm and Meredith Towne were about the same age as Jack and Teal. They were dressed the same too, but there the similarities ended. Kevin was short and thin. In fact, thin described everything about him, from his thin frame to his thin brown hair to his thin voice when he uttered, "Hey, man," following Jack's introduction. He followed that with a thin giggle and a nervous shrug. Kevin Calm didn't seem all that calm.

Meredith contrasted with Teal as much as Kevin did with Jack. Where Teal's every feature summoned the word "straight," Meredith was shorter and her features seemed to summon the word round. She wasn't fat, just round, from her round face to cheery dumpling breasts to a round little tummy to dimpled knees. Even her brown, tightly curled hair gave her head the look of a large round sponge. Meredith stood at Kevin's side, holding his arm, as Teal held Jack's. They looked to be couples.

Gabby stood before the four of them, wanting to go in the house and put on pants, but first he had to find out what they were up to. "You still haven't told me your business."

"Yes, I have." Jack Sand gestured toward the barn. "Like I said, we just have to be here. It's like gravity, man. This is the center of the universe, and we were, like, pulled here."

Gabby eyed them suspiciously. "I reckon you're Sphinx fans then?"

"Fan doesn't cut it, man. We're more like disciples."

Gabby was troubled by the word "disciple" as much as Jack Sand apparently was by the word *fan*.

"And you came all the way from New York?"

"Nonstop, man."

"Just to see…" Now Gabby gestured at the barn. "…*that?*"

Jack Sand shook his head. "Do you know what *that* is, man?"

Gabby suspected a trick question, and he didn't answer right away, and when he did, it was with a questioning tone. "A burnt barn?"

Now all four shook their heads. "Man, you just don't get it," said Jack Sand. "You live at the center of the universe—you own it, man—and you still don't know what you got."

Gabby waited to be told what he had.

"This…this is a shrine, man," said Jack Sand. "That's what it is, a shrine. It's a holy place, and we've come to, like, worship."

Gabby nodded slowly as he pondered the religious significance of his barn. "Well…how long you figure on worshiping?"

Jack Sand looked to the others and then back to Gabby. "We *have* come a long way, you know, and now that we're here, we'd like to stay a while."

"How long's a while?"

Jack Sand shrugged. "Three, four days?"

Gabby had been thinking more in terms of hours. "This ain't a camp-ground, you know."

"And we're not campers. This is a shrine, and we've come to worship. That's all. We won't cause you any trouble, man."

Gabby pondered again. He didn't want them around. Their worship talk made him nervous, and he didn't want to do anything that might encourage more of their kind to come around. But on the other hand, they had come all the way from New York, and it seemed like bad manners to just run them off.

"You can stay till noon," he said.

Jack Sand looked again at the others, all of whom shrugged, and then said, "Okay, man, if that's the best you'll do, we'll take it. We'd like to stay longer, but you're the boss."

Gabby nodded. "And now if you'll excuse me, I reckon I'll go in and put my pants on."

"Aw," said Meredith. "I kinda like the boots and boxer thing. It's kinky."

Gabby turned and hurried for the house.

*   *   *   *

Gabby busied himself most of the morning in the steel building, doing combine maintenance that didn't need doing for another month, because from there he could keep an eye on Jack Sand and company. They still made him nervous, though they didn't do a lot, and what they did do didn't look much like worship. Mostly they sat cross-legged on the ground, facing the charred timbers of the barn. A boom box on the ground between them and the barn blared rock music that didn't seem particularly worshipful either. One of the songs, one that was repeated every half hour or so, sounded vaguely familiar to Gabby, then he recognized it as the tune sung by the mob that had trampled his corn, though the words coming from the boom box were as indistinct as the mob's had been.

At eleven o'clock, they placed a small charcoal grill next to the boom box, raising Gabby's suspicions. They hardly had time for a barbecue if they were to leave by noon, but as it turned out, a barbecue wasn't what they had in mind. Instead, they gathered charred chunks of wood from the barn and kindled them into a small fire, and when the flames licked a foot high, Teal Osborne sprinkled something into the fire. Suddenly, the flames licked higher and shaded from red to green to blue and then back to green again. Gabby viewed this with more suspicion than he had a barbecue. The temperature was well into the eighties now and a recreational fire seemed a bad idea. When they were still adding wood at eleven thirty, he decided it was time to remind them of their noon departure. He had just stepped from the steel building to do so when H. Landon Beard's Cadillac drove into the yard.

H. Landon climbed from his car and walked toward Gabby, though he kept glancing toward the camper and the people squatted on the ground. He wore the same suspenders and bow tie as the day before, but now he was coatless because of the heat. As he came to a stop in front of Gabby, he nodded at the camper.

"What the hell's going on, Gabriel? Looks like a bunch of hippies."

Gabby just shrugged. Jack Sand and company lacked the leather fringe and beads he'd always associated with hippies. Besides, it'd been some time since he'd heard the term, and he wasn't even sure there were such people as hippies anymore.

"Well, who are they?" H. Landon persisted.

Gabby thought a moment. "Shriners, I reckon."

"Shriners! Don't look like Shriners to me. Shriners are those old guys with funny hats that do figure-eights on motorcycles."

"These are a different kind."

H. Landon frowned and then shrugged and opened the leather folio he'd been carrying. "You need to sign this, Gabriel."

Gabby looked at it warily. "What is it?"

"A letter of agreement naming me as your attorney in this Sphinx business." H. Landon took a pen from his shirt pocket and held it out. "It's just a formality. We agreed on everything in principle yesterday."

"Bullshit! We didn't agree on nothing. And I told you yesterday that I don't need a lawyer."

"Now, Gabriel, of course you do. There's a lot of money to be had in all this, and it won't cost you a cent either. I only get paid when we win, and then you get to keep two-thirds of everything. Two-thirds, Gabriel!" H. Landon jabbed a finger at the appropriate place on the letter of agreement. "See?"

Gabby was on the verge of bad manners, but he was distracted by a sudden blast from the Shriners' boom box.

H. Landon pointed in their direction. "You want me to get rid of those hippie dipshits for you, Gabriel?"

"No. I don't want you doing a damn thing. I just want—"

"It'll be my first act as your attorney, and it won't cost you a cent."

Before Gabby could protest, H. Landon strode across the yard and came to a stop squarely in front of the Shriners.

"Turn that off!" he barked, pointing at the boom box.

Kevin Calm scooted on hands and knees to the boom box and turned it off. The others stared in the sudden silence at the looming bulk before them.

"I'm Mr. Cox's attorney," said H. Landon, "and I'm ordering you from the premises."

The Shriners looked questioningly at each other and then at Gabby, who had followed behind H. Landon.

"But it's not noon yet," said Jack Sand.

"Noon is not relevant here," stated H. Landon. "You've been ordered to leave now. If you do not promptly comply with that order, you will face the penalties for trespass."

Jack Sand looked to Gabby again. "Is that square with you, Mr. Cox?"

"No, it ain't!" said Gabby, surprising himself with the raw anger in his voice. "The only one going anywhere is you!" He jabbed a finger at H. Landon.

"But, Gabriel—"

"Get your ass outta here or face the penalties for trespass!" Gabby took a menacing step toward the lawyer.

H. Landon backed toward his car. "You're making a big mistake, Gabriel. I can make you a lot of money, and what'll these people do for you? Hell, they're probably dope heads. They'll rob you blind."

"These people drove a long way to get here, and I gave 'em permission to camp a few days, and it's none of your business anyway 'cause you ain't my lawyer. Now git!"

H. Landon started to protest again, but Gabby took another menacing step and raised a clenched fist, and at that, H. Landon turned and stumbled for his car, where he paused to shout, "You'll regret this, Cox!" Then he climbed in and sped off, spraying gravel across the yard.

Gabby and the Shriners stood silently for a long moment, exchanging uneasy glances. Then Jack Sand cheered, and the Shriners joined in.

"That was cool," said Jack. "And thanks for letting us camp a few days. We appreciate it, man."

The others nodded their agreement, but Gabby could only shrug. He was wondering what he'd gotten himself into.

CHAPTER 9

▼

"Let me get this straight," said Gwen. "You're letting four total strangers camp in your yard?"

Gabby shrugged. "It was that lawyer's fault. He got me all worked up."

Gwen was sitting at her desk, and Gabby was sitting across from her. Beyond her open office door was the Hayesboro Public Library. The library's hushed quiet and high, arched windows always reminded Gabby of church; in fact, the library had become his church. He came every week, and he looked upon the long rows of books with reverence. The muted whispers calmed his soul, and he always took care to avoid using words like "ain't" when he was there. In contrast, he went to church only at Christmas and Easter. And funerals, of course.

"So exactly who are these people?" asked Gwen.

"They're from New York," said Gabby, as if that were explanation enough.

"And?"

He briefly struggled for words to describe his visitors. "They're...they're Shriners."

Gwen's eyebrows shot up. "You mean with the red hats?"

"No. They're a different kind. They're Sphinx Shriners, I reckon."

Gwen nodded now. "And how is this the lawyer's fault?"

He struggled for words again, trying to describe something he didn't fully understand. "At first I told 'em they could stay till noon and—"

"Who?"

"The Shriners. And they were fine with that, and I was fine with it too, 'cause I didn't really want 'em around, but then about eleven thirty, that H. Landon lawyer fella came around again."

Gabby paused, shaking his head.

"And?"

Gabby shrugged. "And he got all pushy, even worse than yesterday. I kept telling him I didn't need a lawyer, and he just ignored me and kept after me to sign this paper that'd make him my lawyer anyway, and I guess I got pretty mad. Then he went over and started yelling at the Shriners like he already was my lawyer, and that got me even madder, and then it got to seeming like me and the Shriners were on the same side—and that's when I said they could stay a few days."

Gwen suppressed a smile. "So would you like to go back on that now? You can, you know. You're the property owner, after all, and you've a right to change your mind, especially if you see them as a threat. I'm sure Sam Stack would be willing to—"

"No, that's okay. I told 'em they could stay a few days, and I'll stick by it. Besides, I wouldn't say they're threatening. They're kinda odd, that's all. They're…they're…"

Words failed Gabby again.

"They're Sphinx fans?" offered Gwen.

"Yeah." Gabby thought to mention Jack Sand's claim that they were disciples but decided against it.

"And that brings us to the reason you're here." Gwen opened a file folder on her desk. "I got that information together on your new friend, Sphinx."

"He's no friend of mine."

"Sorry. Bad joke." She suppressed another smile and then read from a handwritten sheet of paper. "Sphinx was thirty years old. He was born Randy Fisher in Tulsa, Oklahoma."

"Wonder why he changed it to Sphinx?" said Gabby. "Randy Fisher seems like a good enough name to me."

"Not for a rock star." Gwen read on. "He started singing in a band when he was in high school, and in his senior year, he dropped out of both school and the band and tried to make it on his own as a solo musician. For two years, he was pretty much a wannabe, playing bars and roadhouses for nickels and dimes and living on beer and pot. His first break came when he got the opening act for Saturday's Sinners."

"Who?"

"Saturday's Sinners. A rock band. They were pretty big for a while, especially in the South, and Sphinx getting their opening act was literally a break of sorts. Seems the guy that was supposed to open for them broke his leg the day before the tour started, and Sphinx was available, so he sort of fell into the job. That was his first break, and it led to his big break, which was a recording contract, and after a couple duds, he got his first hit."

"He was a pretty good singer, then?"

"So, so," said Gwen, "but then a great voice has never been essential in rock 'n' roll. Mostly, he hit a chord, a nerve, and that led to something of a cult following."

Gabby recalled Jack Sand's use of the word "disciple" again.

"What kinda nerve?"

Gwen thought a moment. "Maybe the best way to answer that is to let you hear some of his music." She held up a plastic CD case. "And I just happen to have some."

She slipped the CD into a CD player on the credenza behind her desk and reached for the play button but then paused. "Perhaps you should close the door. Sphinx music isn't all that appropriate to library decorum."

Gabby closed the door, and Gwen started the CD. In a moment, shrill electric guitar music filled the room, and soon a raspy voice joined in:

Baby, baby, come ride my cloud,
We'll slip the Earth and fly so proud,
We'll soar so high; we'll have it all,
Higher and higher and higher,
So high that we can never fall.

Gwen pushed the pause button. "This is 'Cloud Rider.' It was Sphinx's biggest hit. I guess you could say it's his signature song."

Gabby recognized the tune as the one the Shriners had played over and over, the same tune the mob had sung in his barnyard, and now in Gwen Todd's office, he could make out the words for the first time.

"I reckon he liked flying pretty much."

"I suppose," said Gwen, "but there's more to it than that. Flying's a euphemism here, a metaphor."

Gabby had no idea what a euphemism was, and although he'd heard the term "metaphor," he wasn't sure what it meant, so he simply nodded.

Gwen pushed the play button.

Baby, baby, come ride my cloud,
We'll slip the Earth and its smothering shroud,
Breathe this cloud, this fog so sweet,
Higher and higher and higher,
They all are small beneath our feet.

Gwen paused the CD again. "It's pretty much understood that 'this fog so sweet' is marijuana. Sphinx was into pot big time, not to mention an assortment of drugs and booze on top of all that." She pushed the play button.

Baby, baby, come ride my cloud,
We'll slip the Earth and its pissed-off crowd,
So spread your legs on this cloud so soft,
Higher and higher and higher,
And I'll fill you as we soar aloft.
Baby, baby, come ride my cloud,
My cloud, my cloud,
Baby, baby, spread on my cloud,
My cloud, my cloud,
Come ride my cloud, my cloud, my cloud.

The guitar music faded, and Gwen pushed the stop button. "There you have it: Sphinx, pretty well summed up in three verses. Counterculture, drugs, and sex, the basics of any good rock star."

Gabby picked up the plastic CD case. Sphinx was pictured on the cover, standing before an array of psychedelic colors, holding an electric guitar by its neck at his side. His pants were skintight and low-slung and colored silver to match his boots. His black shirt was aglitter with sequins and unbuttoned to his waist, revealing a taut chest and belly. His smile was more of a sneer, but it was Sphinx's hair that grabbed Gabby's attention. It was blonde, platinum blonde, and fell below his shoulders, and an airplane roared into Gabby's thoughts with a flash of blonde hair in the cockpit window.

He put the CD case down on the desk. "Wonder what brung a fella like that to my farm?"

"Like I said yesterday, pure chance."

Gabby shook his head. "I could maybe buy it was pure chance that he flew out this way, and maybe if he had engine trouble and crashed into my barn, that might be pure chance too, but he buzzed me three times. Where's the chance in that?"

"We may never know why he did that, Gabriel. Then again, we might. The NTSB hasn't released any findings yet, but given Sphinx's history with drugs, I wouldn't be surprised if that doesn't eventually explain some of this."

"You think he was high on something?"

Gwen shrugged. "Who knows? But the thing to keep in mind is that as far as Sphinx was concerned, you were a complete stranger. No one can recall him ever being in this area, and you know that the two of you never met. He knew nothing about you, Gabriel, so the fact that he crashed into your barn, whether he buzzed it or not, is purely coincidental."

Gabby looked down at Sphinx's picture again, as if it might somehow provide answers. After a moment he changed the subject.

"What about the woman?"

"Sparkle?"

He nodded.

Gwen took another sheet of paper from the file. "There're lots of words that describe Sparkle: beautiful, rich, spoiled, silly, narcissistic—and those are just for starters."

"But she wasn't a rock star; that's what that fed said. He said she was just a wannabe."

Gwen thought a moment. "I don't know that I'd call her a wannabe, either. A wannabe is at least trying to be something. Sparkle may've had some potential talent, but there's no evidence she ever tried to develop it. She was just out for a good time. And she loved the limelight. If she had a talent for anything, it was getting her face in front of a camera." Gwen paused and smiled. "And sometimes she got other parts of her body in front of a camera too."

The airplane roared into Gabby's thoughts again with its flash of blonde hair, followed by the image of a naked man and a naked woman in the cockpit.

"Is…was Sparkle her real name?"

Gwen shook her head and read from her notes. "Born Taylor Welling-ton. She was twenty-four years old."

It occurred to Gabby that Sparkle had traded two last names for a single first name, an odd one at that, and he wondered why people didn't name girls Mary anymore.

Gwen read on. "Her father owns Planet Wellington, the big hotel casino complex in Las Vegas. She was an only child. She grew up amid glitter and excess with far too much money to ever develop any character, so I suppose it's no surprise that she spent all her time cavorting in the shallow end of the pop culture pool."

Gabby judged by Gwen's tone as much as by her words that she held Sparkle in low regard.

"She broke on the national scene four years ago when she dated Dirk Dean."

"Who's Dirk Dean?"

"A Hollywood hunk. A so-so actor, but he gets a lot play in the star magazines, and that meant Sparkle got a lot of play too, which she loved, of course." Gwen looked at her notes again. "She and Sphinx had been an item for the last year or so. It was an on-and-off thing, which almost seemed staged. They'd do something outlandish in public, and the magazines would all do a story. Then they'd break up. Another story. Then they'd get back together. Yet another story, and so on. It was sort of like Cinderella and Prince Charming rolled together with Bonnie and Clyde."

"So...do you have a picture of her?" Gabby had seen Sparkle on TV often in recent days, but now for some reason, he couldn't summon her face. Only blonde hair, an exposed navel, and cleavage came to mind.

Gwen took a news clipping from her file and slid it across the desk. Sparkle was pictured next to a pool, wearing a brief bikini, and Gabby realized why her face hadn't registered, as those other features captured his gaze. Now he studied her face. Her eyes and nose and mouth were regular enough, a lack of flaws that might pass for beauty, but at that moment, the camera had captured a sullen pout that urged the eye away again, back to hair, navel, and breasts.

"She was pretty," he said. "Too bad she hadda die so young."

Gwen shrugged. "Life in the fast lane'll do that to you."

Gabby found Gwen's lack of sympathy for youthful death to be strangely out of character, and an awkward silence hung in the room until he said, "Well, reckon I oughta be going. Thanks for getting all that information for me."

She put everything back in the file and slid it across the desk. "Take it along if you like. I just hope it's helpful in some way."

Gabby looked warily at the file and then picked it up. "I guess it does help to know a little about 'em."

They both stood, and Gwen said, "I'll be going out to check on Dad later. Would you like me to drop off some more sweet corn?"

"Sure. That'd be great...if it's not to much trouble."

"No trouble." She smiled. "Besides, you've gotten my curiosity up about your Shriners. It'll give me a chance to check them out."

Gabby frowned at the mention of the Shriners, but then he surprised her by saying, "Maybe you could bring enough corn for them too? If it's not too much trouble?"

"No trouble at all. And that's very considerate of you, Gabriel."

"Well, I am sorta their host."

"I hope they remember that."

"Whaddaya mean?"

"I hope they remember that you're their host and that they're your guests and that they should behave like guests. After all, it *was* Sphinx fans that ran amok on your farm and trampled your corn."

Gabby cocked his head as he considered this. "I reckon the Shriners are different."

Gabby left, and Gwen turned back to the work on her desk, but she had trouble concentrating. Her mind kept wandering to thoughts of Sphinx and Sparkle, to thoughts of the fast lane, and then inevitably back to California.

CHAPTER 10

▼

Tess Snow became the focus of Gwen Todd's job. The country singer turned actress was shooting the second movie of a three-movie contract, and Gwen was charged with ensuring that Tess upheld her end of the deal. It wasn't easy. The first movie had been a box office hit and Tess had received good reviews, but instead of encouraging her to reach higher still with her next effort, that success seemed only to make her more self-centered.

Gwen's days alternated between indulging Tess's whims and herding her away from those whims forbidden by the Chrome Agency (drugs and booze during working hours). She was able to get Tess to work sober most days only by showing up at Tess's house each morning at five to brew coffee and then escort her to the studio. Those early morning visits gave Gwen extra insight into Tess, insight she didn't really want, such as details of Tess's sex life.

Hector the pool boy turned out to be only the tip of the iceberg, and Gwen arrived apprehensively each morning, wondering what new combination she might find in Tess's bed. Tess's appetite was huge, and her taste ran with equal gusto to either sex, sometimes to both at the same time. Gwen never accepted her own invitation to climb into Tess's bed, though it was repeated a time or two. She had no leanings in that direction, and even if she had, the Chrome Agency had a strict rule forbidding any liaison between associates and clients. Even the boss, Ron Chrome, adamantly followed the rule.

"Never sleep with your product, Toddy," he said. "Do it just once, and they get ideas. They think they're your equal all of a sudden."

Chrome showed no such restraint when it came to his associates, however, and Gwen had been at the agency only two months when she found herself in his bed one night. It was the night of the Academy Awards. Gwen and Chrome had herded Tess to the ceremony in a rented ten-thousand-dollar dress, and after the awards, they herded her to a few of the many parties, where Tess drank too much and tore the dress. That mishap aside, they got Tess safely home by midnight, then Chrome and Gwen stopped for a drink, which led to another drink, which led to Chrome's bed—he had just divorced wife number three. It happened just that one time, and to Gwen it felt like business, though it didn't make her feel any more his equal. She felt only that her indoctrination into the firm was now complete.

Apart from being hustled by Tess and bedded by her boss, Gwen's love life was much to her liking, mostly because the town was full of handsome young wannabe actors who saw Gwen Todd as a way to land a Chrome contract. She knew they were attempting to use her, but she also knew that their attempts would fail, and because she was more or less using them too, it all seemed okay in a California sort of way. They were a succession of pretty boys who stopped at every mirror, but Gwen was twenty-two and living in Tinsel Town, and she soon found out that pretty boys could be fun. That's all it was: fun, never serious, and the relationships were always brief. Seth Rawlings was the only exception, but that's not to say that he and Gwen had a serious relationship, only that they came closer to one than she did with the others.

Seth was tall, well-built, and beach-boy handsome with startling blue eyes. He had grown up in Southern California with the dream of becoming an actor, and he pursued that dream by doing two hundred push-ups and running six miles each day. Push-ups and running were his strategy for everything. From time to time, he had tried acting lessons too, but those confused him and sapped his confidence, whereas push-ups and running always hyped his confidence. In her kinder moments, Gwen thought Seth vulnerable. In her less kind moments, she thought him just plain dumb, but vulnerable or dumb, Seth was always easy on the eyes. And, of course, fun.

Seth was strictly a wannabe, his career was going nowhere, and between push-ups and running and auditioning for bit parts, there was little time left for a job, so he lived on the brink of poverty. His circumstances improved some when he moved into Gwen's apartment with a promise to pay half the rent, a promise he seldom kept, but he made up for that by doing their laundry and much of the cooking. At first, he surprised Gwen with his skill in the kitchen, then she learned that, like many wannabe actors, he had worked in several restaurants. There were no surprises in the bedroom, though; Seth was an able and proud lover.

One night, after making love, he turned on his side and propped his head on his hand as he stroked Gwen's hip with his other hand. "You're great," he said.

"You're not so bad yourself."

"I love you."

"I love you too."

They'd taken to professing their love about a week ago, and Gwen was fairly certain that his insincerity matched her own.

His hand moved to her breast. "Did you talk to Mr. Chrome?"

She hesitated. She'd known this was coming. It'd become part of their routine: foreplay, sex, then Ron Chrome.

His hand moved to her other breast. "Well?"

"No, Seth, there just hasn't been a good time."

"But I need an agent, Gwen. It's the only way I'm ever gonna make it. You gotta have an agent in this town."

"Maybe...maybe you should try one of the bigger agencies."

He withdrew his hand. "You saying I'm not good enough for Chrome, is that it?"

"No, Seth, but we're a small agency—you know that. We only have six clients right now, and I don't think Ron's looking to add any. And it's not about how good you are. It's just that our clients are established. They have credentials."

He pushed the sheet back. "This isn't a credential?"

"Seth—"

He took her hand and held it to his chest. "I worked damn hard to get this body."

"Yes, Seth, I know, and you look great—you really do—but you need more. You know that. And we've talked about all this before. You…you need a résumé."

"That's screwy, Gwen. Don't you see what you're saying? You're saying I need a résumé to get an agent, but I also need to get some good parts in order to put a résumé together, and I can't get any good parts without an agent. It's like a goddamn catch-22."

Suddenly, he laughed out loud and moved her hand to his crotch. "Maybe I got one good part." He laughed again. "Won't do me any good, though, since I don't wanna star in some fuck flick. Harrison Ford didn't get where he is doing fuck flicks."

Gwen sighed. Seth's goal was to be the next Harrison Ford, and she'd carefully avoided telling him what she thought of his chances.

"Look, just ask Chrome, okay? So he says no. Then fine, it's no, but maybe on your recommendation, he'll say yes. We'll never know if you don't ask."

Gwen sighed again. She knew what Ron Chrome's answer would be. And she knew he would see any request on behalf of her boyfriend to be inexcusably unprofessional, but she also doubted that Seth would give it up. Now, making matters worse, he gave her his best boyish smile as his good part grew in her hand.

"I'll talk to him tomorrow," she said.

His smile widened, and he pulled her close and kissed her. He whispered in her ear, "As long as we've waited this long, let's wait till next week. I've got some new glossies coming."

*   *   *   *

California memories nagged Gwen all that day, and at four o'clock, she gave up on work and left the library to drive out to her father's farm. What she found there was enough finally to jar her thoughts from the past.

L. R. Todd was seated at the kitchen table when she walked in. That was normal enough, but nothing else was. All the windows were closed, the air conditioning was off, and it was over eighty degrees inside the house—and L. R. was wearing his heavy camouflage hunting coat. Sweat streamed down his face, but he seemed not to notice as he focused on cleaning and oiling the twelve-gauge shotgun on the table.

"What are you doing, Dad?"

"Getting ready."

"For what? Hunting season's months away. And besides, you haven't hunted in years."

"Them goddamn city folks've been in my sweet corn."

"Are you sure?"

L. R. nodded. "Dave at the gas station told me."

"Well, Dad, how would Dave know that? Are you sure he wasn't talking about some of the cannery's fields? People get into those all the time, but your little patch is so isolated. They'd have to come through the yard to get to it."

L. R.'s bushy black eyebrows knitted in a moment's confusion, then he turned back to wiping the gun with an oily rag. "Dave told me."

Gwen's stomach knotted. Her father's confusion was one thing, but that confusion coupled with a shotgun was quite another thing.

"I'm sure you're wrong, Dad. You must've misunderstood Dave. And I think having a gun out is a bad idea. There could be an accident. And you should take that coat off before you get overheated."

L. R.'s eyebrows knitted again at his daughter's opinions and demands, and Gwen took advantage of his confusion to grab the gun.

"I'll put this in the basement," she said. "I'm going down there to start a load of laundry anyway."

L. R. stared at the spot on the table where the gun had been. "But Dave—"

"Dave's wrong, Dad. But after I start the laundry, I'll go out and check your patch. I can tell if someone's been in there. People who steal sweet corn are always in a hurry, and they knock down a lot of stalks."

This seemed to satisfy L. R. "Pick some for yourself while you're out there."

"I intend to. And I'll get some more for Gabriel too."

L. R. nodded. "Good. Gabby's a neighbor. That's who the corn's for. Neighbors. Not goddamn city folks."

Gwen didn't mention that she would pick extra corn for the "city folks" from New York camping in Gabby's yard. Nor did she mention when she came up from the basement that she'd put the shotgun away behind a crate under the stairs instead of in the cabinet where L. R. kept his hunting gear. She had also searched that cabinet for shotgun shells, thinking she would take those with her, but she found none. She hoped that meant there were none.

CHAPTER 11

▼

Banished to Hayesboro. That was the recurring thought dogging Tanner Mills as he drove through the countryside that afternoon. It'd been a hell of a week. He'd gone from his regular beat at the state capitol to his editor's doghouse and now to banishment in Hayesboro. And what pissed him off most was that his editor had OK'd the story that got him in trouble. In fact, it'd been his editor's idea in the first place to write about the governor's son getting caught in a St. Paul whorehouse raid, and now Tanner was the one being punished.

"You're not being punished," his editor had said.

"You don't call a week in Hayesboro punishment?"

"I call it a cooling-off period. Damn it, Tanner, face the facts. You can't be effective over at the capitol if neither the governor nor any of his staff'll talk to you. Just give them some time to get over it; then you can go back."

"So now journalism's a popularity contest, huh? Funny, I always thought it had something to do with the First Amendment."

His editor slammed his coffee mug down, splashing a few drops onto his desk. "Don't get on your fucking high horse with me, Tanner. You presume to lecture me on the First Amendment again, and I'll ship your ass to Hayesboro for a month."

"But don't you see what you're doing? You're letting them decide who writes the paper, for chrissakes. Next thing you know, they'll wanna write our goddamn editorials."

His editor took three deliberate breaths before responding.

"Just once, Tanner, just once, would you not make a federal case outta everything? And the governor has a point. This isn't about his policies or even his conduct. It's a family matter, and he's entitled to some privacy in family matters. Put yourself in the governor's shoes for once."

"It's not my job to wear his shoes. It's my job to smell his feet when he takes 'em off. And besides, it's not strictly a family matter. It's also about the cozy treatment his kid got from the St. Paul cops, and that *is* the public's business."

His editor held up his hands. "Okay, Tanner, I'll concede you that much. You're the protector of truth and motherhood and the goddamn Constitution, but you're still going to Hayesboro for a week. You'll interview folks. You'll get the small-town take on rock stars dropping outta the goddamn sky. You'll write a nice feature. And by God, you'll let this thing blow over so we can all get back to work."

"But I'm a political writer, not a feature writer. If you really want this goddamn story, and I suspect you don't, then send one of your sob sisters out there."

This time, his editor actually broke his mug, and coffee splattered across his desk and onto Tanner's lap. The editor then aimed a menacing finger.

"One more word outta you, Tanner, and you'll be writing fucking obituaries for a year!"

Now as Tanner drove through the warm July afternoon, he was surrounded on both sides by cornfields. He hated cornfields. Cornfields were boring. There wasn't any news in cornfields. He was a city guy. All the action was in the city. Well, there wasn't going to be much action for the next week—of that he was certain—and making matters worse, his girlfriend had moved out of his apartment the night before.

"It's not working, Tanner," she'd said. "You're just not ready for commitment."

So his editor thought him too committed, and his girlfriend thought him not committed enough, and they were both out to punish him. It'd been a hell of a week. And it was only going to get worse.

CHAPTER 12

▼

Gabby couldn't remember the last time he'd been to a party. It might've been his twelfth birthday, but that recollection was vague. The Coxes had never been party people; parties had always seemed...what? Immodest? But the gathering on Gabby's porch that evening didn't seem that way at all. Actually, it seemed magical, and Gabby guessed that was due in part to the spontaneity with which it had begun and in part to the youthful contrast provided by the Shriners. Then, too, the fact that Gwen Todd was still there was more magic than Gabby had imagined in some time.

Gwen had arrived in the late afternoon with a gunnysack full of sweet corn, and he had introduced her to the Shriners. Common courtesies had been observed, and pleasantries had been exchanged. Then the group had husked the corn, and from that hands-on act, a party had germinated. They made a trip to town for beer and brats and buns. Gabby fired up his charcoal grill on the lawn next to the porch for the brats. Gwen, Teal, and Meredith took over the kitchen, where they brought a cauldron of water to boil for the corn, easily finding numerous things to discuss. Gabby, Jack, and Kevin stood around the grill, drinking beer, watching the red glow spread through the pile of charcoal, and uttering the guarded things men utter when they drink beer and watch charcoal.

Now it was dark. They were sitting on the floor of the porch, leaning back against wall or railing. Gabby had offered to bring chairs out from the kitchen, but the Shriners had opted for the floor, so Gabby and Gwen had joined them, and the two rocking chairs stood empty. Dirty plates, a mustard jar, a saltshaker, and the short remains of a pound of butter cluttered the floor, and at the center of the clutter, a plastic wastebasket was heaped with corncobs. Jack had moved the camper closer, and it now stood just twenty feet from the porch. From the camper, Teal and Meredith had produced a string of colored lights, which now hung between the camper and the porch, adding to the festive mood.

More beers were opened to be sipped slowly, and as they settled into after-dinner contentment, Jack stood. "Mind if we smoke?" he asked Gabby.

Gabby shrugged. He wasn't a smoker, but they were outside, and he didn't want to do anything that might dampen the party. "Go ahead," he said.

Jack went to the camper and returned a moment later with what looked to be a small, round cookie tin, and only when he took a joint from the tin and put it between his lips did Gabby realize what Jack intended to smoke. Jack lit the joint and inhaled deeply, holding the smoke in his lungs for a long moment before exhaling with a satisfied smile. Then he held the joint out to Gabby. "Breathe this cloud, this fog so sweet?"

Gabby was briefly confused, but then he recognized the words from Sphinx's song and understood. "No thanks," he said.

"But you're okay with it, right?"

"Sure."

"Because you're the boss, man. What you say goes."

Gabby shook his head. "I don't mind. Go ahead."

Jack grinned and passed the joint to Teal. "That's cool, man, because nothing rounds out the night like a little dope."

Gabby really didn't mind, and now as another joint was lit to be passed around, he realized that his approval had as much to do with where they were as it had to do with what was being done. They were on his farm, his land, and on his land Gabby got to decide what the law was. His father had always said that if a man had enough land, he could go by whatever law he chose, so long as it didn't harm a neighbor, even a distant and unseen one. Well, Gabby knew that wasn't exactly true, and it became less true with each passing year, as more and more laws from St. Paul and Washington dictated what a farmer could and couldn't do on his land. Still, there were times, times like this night, when he could act out his father's belief. This night, he was both Congress and Supreme Court of three hundred and fifty acres on the Minnesota prairie, and as such, he had legalized marijuana. It was the law. On his porch, anyway. Besides, he didn't see how smoking a little pot would hurt anyone there, much less distant and unseen neighbors who ought to mind their own business. No, Gabby didn't mind the Shriners smoking pot, but he was more than a little surprised when Meredith passed a joint to Gwen, and Gwen took it and expertly inhaled.

"You don't talk much for a guy named Gabby."

Teal Osborne's comment shook Gabby from his lawmaker reverie, as well as from his surprise at Gwen Todd, pot-smoking librarian, and he blushed as everyone turned to him.

"Don't have much to say," he said with a shrug. He'd been enjoying their clever banter, but now that enjoyment gave way to regret at his own inability to say clever things. Then, to his surprise, something clever came to him, and he blurted it out. "How come they named you after a duck?" he asked Teal.

Both Jack and Kevin laughed, but Teal didn't see the humor. She was sitting next to Jack, and she punched his shoulder with a small fist. Then she turned to Gabby. "I'm *not* named after a duck. Teal also happens to be a color."

"It is?" Gabby's palette didn't go far beyond the primary colors.

"Yes. It's, like, blue-green. And very stylish, I might add."

Jack snickered. "That can be your nickname. Blue Green Osborne. Very stylish indeed."

Teal punched his shoulder again. "At least my name's more imaginative than, say, *John*."

Jack grimaced. "My name's Jack."

"Jack's your nickname, *John Jr.*" She punched his shoulder a third time.

"Look, it's not my fault that my parents were too damn dull to think up a different name. Besides, I took care of that myself. The name's Jack. And stop punching me."

Gabby, fearing his attempt at cleverness had started a fight, tried to change the subject. "What does your father do?" he asked.

"Mine?" said Jack.

Gabby nodded.

"Wall Street. He's an *investment banker.*"

The disapproval in Jack's tone was evident, but at least he wasn't arguing with Teal, so Gabby pursued his line of questioning. "How 'bout your father, Teal? What's he do?"

"Wall Street too. Only he's a lawyer. And what's with the daddy quiz? We have mothers too. Don't you, like, wanna know what our mothers do?"

Gabby felt himself spiraling into deeper and deeper trouble, and his mouth quit working, but Gwen came to his rescue.

"He doesn't mean anything by it, Teal. It's a guy thing, that's all. So what does your mother do?"

"She drinks."

Jack chuckled. "Wish mine did. Then maybe she'd get off my ass."

The conversation stalled briefly, and then Gwen asked, "What about your parents, Kevin?"

Kevin shrugged. "They're split. Mom got the condo in Florida. Dad's on Madison Avenue. Advertising." He inhaled the joint just passed to him and giggled as he exhaled. "And he'd give Jack's dad and Teal's dad an argument over who works on the more powerful street."

All the Shriners laughed at that, easing the tension, and joints were passed again.

"I guess that leaves your family, Meredith," said Gwen.

Meredith exhaled and passed a joint. "My father's the most powerful of all. He's got God on his side."

The Shriners laughed again, and Kevin explained. "Her dad's a Methodist minister."

"Actually, my father's in the same business as Kevin's," Meredith added. "The half-truth business. The manipulation business."

That hung in the air for an awkward moment, until Gwen broke the silence again. "Do you all live right in New York?"

Teal shook her head. "We're all from, like, White Plains."

"And what do the four of you do in White Plains?"

"Go to college," said Teal. "Junior college, actually."

"Yale wanted me, of course," said Jack, "but I decided not to waste the old man's money."

"Yale. Right." Teal laughed. "It's junior college for Junior."

Jack glowered, but before he and Teal could resume squabbling, Gwen changed the subject again. "That's a nice camper. Whose is it?"

"Mine," said Jack.

"His daddy's, actually," said Teal.

Jack shrugged. "Yeah, well, they're in Europe for the month, but I'm sure he'd be happy to know we're seeing the country and expanding our horizons."

"Why here?" asked Gwen. "Why not someplace fun like Florida?"

"Oh, this isn't a vacation," said Teal. "It's a spiritual thing. We're, like, pilgrims, you know?"

Gwen smiled at the mention of pilgrims but said nothing.

"It's the Sphinx thing, you see," said Teal. "We're into Sphinx, like, in a spiritual way."

"Yeah," said Jack, "and when he crashed, it was, like wow, a real downer. We were having a bad time with it, and then we decided, what the hell, let's get in the camper and go."

"Follow the spirit, that's what we did," said Teal. "We followed the spirit to the spot where it went full circle."

Gwen raised her eyebrows. "Full circle?"

"Yeah," said Teal. "We didn't get it at first, either. That's why we were so down, I think. His death just seemed so senseless, but then we saw it, the Jesus thing, and, like wow, everything made sense."

"Jesus thing?"

"Well, yeah," said Teal. "Jesus was born in a barn, wasn't he?"

"So?"

"So Sphinx died in a barn. You have to think about it, I guess, but when you do, it really hits you. It's circular, see? The circle, like, always comes back to where it started from."

Gwen smiled despite her effort to contain it. "And you're suggesting there's some connection between Sphinx and Jesus?"

"Of course not." This from Meredith in a dismissive tone.

"We're not?" said Teal.

Meredith gave her a disapproving look. "You have to excuse Teal. She makes these little metaphysical leaps sometimes."

Teal started to say something but sulked against Jack's shoulder instead.

Meredith turned to Gwen. "It's kinda hard to explain how we feel about Sphinx, but I think in a way, it really is spiritual. His music is so real. It touches us in a spiritual way. It's not phony like...like Wall Street or Madison Avenue. Or even the Methodist Church."

"Yeah," said Teal, reentering the conversation. "Sphinx's music teaches us to, like, live our lives and to love each other, and that's like Jesus, isn't it?"

Another sidelong disapproving glance from Meredith, and then Gwen asked, "What about Sparkle? How does she fit into all this?"

"She's Sphinx's Mary Magdalene," said Teal without hesitation.

"Don't go there, Teal," said Meredith.

Gabby had been struggling to keep up with the drift of conversation, and now the image of Sphinx and Sparkle, naked in the cockpit the moment before crashing into the barn, popped into his head, then it popped out again as a loud engine sounded from the driveway. A moment later, a pickup on oversized tires rumbled into the yard and came to a stop next to the Shriners' camper.

"Oh, hell," muttered Gabby, recognizing Slade Walters. The crop duster who often disturbed Gabby's peace had now appeared to disturb Gabby's party.

Slade climbed from the cab. He wore jeans and cowboy boots and a Western-style shirt. He was only a few years older than the Shriners, but his long, shaggy hair and beard and his bulging gut made the difference in age seem greater. He held a beer bottle in his hand. "Looks like we're having us a party," he said and lurched toward the porch.

"Whatcha want, Slade?" asked Gabby warily.

Slade ignored him, leaned against the porch railing, and leered at Teal, sitting three feet away. "Well, now, ain't you a pretty thing with them long legs and all?"

Jack sat up, and Gabby spoke again, an edge in his voice now. "You got no business here, Slade."

Slade leered at Teal a moment longer before turning to Gabby. "Now that ain't very neighborly, neighbor. And I'm just being sociable. I was driving home, minding my own business, and I saw all the pretty lights and figured that you was having a party and that my invitation musta got lost in the mail." Slade chuckled at this and took a long swig of beer.

"Looks like you've already partied enough," said Gabby. "Why don't you just head on home?"

Slade ignored him again and turned back to the Shriners. "Howdy, folks. I'm Slade Walters, Gabby's neighbor from just a mile over. Don't believe I've met you. Guess old Gabby's having himself an outta-towner party, and he don't want folks to know he's got leggy friends." Another chuckle and another swig, and then Slade's expression changed as he sniffed the air. "Say, smells like you folks're smoking some pretty good shit. Ain't that Gabby something. Pot and long legs from outta town. You leading a secret life out here, neighbor?"

Gabby stood. "It's time to leave, Slade."

"Ain't you gonna offer me something to smoke first? That's pretty goddamn rude."

Jack looked uneasily to Gabby, and Gabby took a step toward Slade. "I said leave, Slade."

"What? Just when the party's getting good?" Slade turned to the Shriners again. "See, here's the problem, folks. Old Gabby's just pissed 'cause I fly too low over his farm sometimes. Ain't that right, Gabby? 'Cept he's got no right to be pissed, 'cause all those times I flew over, I might've made a little noise, but I never once crashed into his barn like that Sphinx asshole did."

"Watch what you say, mister," said Teal. "This is a hallowed place."

Slade leered again. "Say, legs can talk." He looked at Jack. "She fuck too?"

Jack was on his feet in a flash. "Shut your mouth, sky cowboy."

"Why don't you try and shut it, punk?" Slade's step up onto the porch was timed perfectly for his nose to meet Jack's flying fist, and in the next instant, Slade was sprawled backward onto the lawn. There, he flopped about, thrashing his arms as he tried to get up, and after a moment, he managed to get to his knees. Blood flowed from his nose. "I'm gonna pound the shit outta you, punk!"

But before Slade could get to his feet, Gabby was down off the porch. He grabbed Slade's beard and held it while he smacked his knee into Slade's forehead. Slade sprawled again, and this time, he didn't flop or thrash.

Gabby stood over him, and Slade blinked up in a daze. "Get outta here, Slade."

Slade blinked again and gently touched his nose and then his forehead, and after another moment, he slowly got to his feet and lumbered like a wounded bear to his pickup, where he paused to glare back at Gabby before climbing into the cab.

As Slade drove from the yard, Gabby turned to the others. "Sorry," was all he could think to say. It no longer felt like a party.

CHAPTER 13

▼

Gabby couldn't sleep. For one thing, it was hot. He lay spread-eagled on his back, wearing only boxers and not so much as a sheet covering him, but the still, sultry air weighed on him like a quilt, and sweat beaded his forehead. Gabby, like his parents before him, had always eschewed air conditioning as a three-month luxury in Minnesota, but nights like this gave him second thoughts. He glanced at the bedside clock: 2:00 AM. He closed his eyes, hoping for sleep, but instead, the image of Slade Walters, sprawled on the lawn, bullied its way into his thoughts. Slade had dogged Gabby's thoughts since the scuffle earlier that night, though it wasn't a matter of intimidation. True, Slade was a bully, but Gabby knew that he only bullied those who allowed themselves to be bullied. No, Gabby didn't fear Slade the bully, but he did fear Slade's mouth. Slade was a blowhard, and Gabby knew that news of the party and the Shriners and the pot-smoking would soon spread through the Legion Club, then through all of Hayesboro. Gabby didn't know what repercussions might come of that, but the thought of it knotted his stomach and conspired with the heat to keep him awake.

Then there was Gwen Todd. He worried that her reputation might be sullied by Slade's gossip, and that kept him awake too, but more than that, his thoughts kept returning to her leave-taking a few hours earlier. The party broke up after Slade left, and Gwen left soon after that. Gabby walked her to her car, where he apologized for Slade's crude behavior. She shrugged and remarked that she'd seen worse, which surprised Gabby. Then she did something that surprised him even more.

She put her hand on his arm. "Don't worry about it," she said, then she rose up on tiptoes and kissed him.

It was a sisterly peck on his cheek, but to Gabby it was like a hundred volts of electricity. And if that weren't enough, when she stretched to kiss him, her breast brushed his arm, and that was like a thousand volts. Now Gabby knew that it was the touch of her lips and the touch of her breast, more than the heat or Slade Walters, that kept sleep at bay.

He glanced at the clock again: 2:03 AM. The night was endless. The night was also cloudless, and the moon was just a day past full, so the room was awash with moonlight. He lay there several minutes more, watching the light play on the walls, and then he sighed and got up and walked to the window.

The Shriners had moved the camper so that it stood near the barn once more, but even at that distance, it was clearly revealed in the moonlight. Gabby stared at it for a time, wondering if it was as hot inside the camper as it was in the house, wondering if the Shriners were able to sleep, wondering....He shook his head to stop his wonderings before they became another thing to keep him awake. He turned back to his bed, but it looked hot, rumpled, and uninviting, and he decided that a shot of whiskey might be the thing to tame his thoughts and wonderings and finally permit sleep.

Downstairs, the kitchen was as moonlit as his bedroom, and he didn't bother turning on lights. He took the whiskey from the cupboard, and after pouring two inches into a tumbler, he reached to put the bottle away, next to the peanut butter, where it was kept. But he changed his mind and left it on the counter instead, musing that two inches might not be enough to subdue this night's thoughts and wonderings.

The first sip burned his throat. The second burned somewhat less, and the third not at all. He moved to the kitchen window and stared out at the yard and scratched his crotch—a morning routine now performed in the dead of night. Then, just as he raised the glass for another sip, he detected motion, the slightest movement, beyond the burnt ruins of the barn, at the very edge of the grove. He lowered the glass and squinted, but now there was nothing, only the dark grove silhouetted against the moonlit sky. He was certain he'd seen something. Could it have been the Shriners? What business could they have in his grove in the middle of the night? Or maybe it was someone else? Perhaps a late-arriving Sphinx fan bent on owning a charred remembrance? Then he saw it again, a flicker of movement, and he focused on the spot; a moment later, he chuckled with relief as a deer, a young doe, walked from the grove into the moonlight.

Gabby watched and sipped as the doe moved soundlessly past the barn and past the Shriners' camper and then came to a stop in the middle of the yard, where it slowly turned its head from side to side, its twitching ears alert for danger in the night. Gabby smiled and knocked back the rest of his whiskey. There had always been deer around the Cox farm. For years, they'd raided his mother's garden, much to her displeasure, but Gabby had always viewed those raids as a necessary cost for filling their freezer with venison sausage each fall. Nor did he keep a garden anymore, so he saw the doe as a welcome visitor, free to chew on anything it chose.

And in light of recent visitors to the Cox farm—naked rock stars, pushy feds, stampeding fans, bullying neighbors—the doe was especially welcome. It was certainly the most normal thing to happen in days, and Gabby took it as a hopeful sign that perhaps things were getting better. The doe's visit, he decided, was worthy of another sip or two of whiskey, and he went to the counter, poured another inch, and then returned to the window. The doe was still there, so motionless it might have passed for a lawn ornament, but suddenly, it jerked its head around, its ears twitching again. In the next instant, it bounded into the air, coming down in a full run across the yard and into the trampled corn. Gabby watched it run in the moonlight for well over a hundred yards before it finally faded into the night. He wondered what had spooked it. He looked around the yard, but all was perfectly still. Then he heard a noise, a metallic click, like the sound of a latch, and in the next moment, two people came into view at the back of the camper.

It was Kevin Calm and Meredith Towne. Gabby recognized them at once by their body shapes: Kevin short and skinny, and Meredith short and round. They walked silently, arms around each other's waist, in the direction of the steel building. After twenty paces or so, they stopped and stood for a moment of indecision, but then they continued on, walking directly to the old hayrack parked next to the toolshed. Hay hadn't been cut on the Cox farm in years, and the rack mostly stood there, its boards weathering in the sun, a flat bed available for moving heavy objects. Gabby had last used it that spring, to haul bags of seed to the field, and it'd been parked next to the shed ever since.

Kevin and Meredith stood by the rack for several moments, face to face, as if in whispered conversation, then they came together in full embrace, their lips joining. Gabby froze, afraid to move. He didn't think they could see him, standing inside the darkened house, but the moonlight seemed suddenly brighter, and he felt exposed, exposed as a voyeur, caught spying on a private and intimate act. He felt shame, but he couldn't take his eyes from the embracing couple. He was also acutely aware of the heat once more, and his mouth went dry, so he risked slowly raising the glass for a sip of whiskey.

The kiss by the hayrack lasted all that sip and another sip, and when it finally ended, Kevin and Meredith climbed onto the rack, where they sat side by side, their legs dangling, their arms circling in a new embrace. Quickly, the embrace grew ardent, their kisses urgent, their hands bold, and Gabby's shame grew with their passion, but still his eyes remained riveted. Kevin began tugging at Meredith's T-shirt, awkwardly and ineffectively until she helped, and then the shirt slid over her head to be tossed aside on the rack. Next, Kevin attacked her bra, deftly now and without assistance, and Meredith's breasts were briefly bared, two pale moons in the moonlight, before being eclipsed by Kevin's hands.

Gabby sipped whiskey, but it did nothing to slow his quickening breath or ease the stirring in his loins. He wasn't a virgin, though at that moment, watching Kevin and Meredith, he felt like one. His shyness had always gotten in the way of relationships. He'd never had sex with a woman for whom he felt anything but lust. He'd never even known their last names. Minneapolis whores had been the limit of his experience, anonymous trips to the city every month or so, trips that brought only relief, never love. In recent years, even that had become more than his shyness could bear, and he now mostly settled for the solitude of masturbation. No, sex had never had anything to do with love, or even friendship, and now envy joined the other emotions raging through Gabby as Kevin's T-shirt was heaped with Meredith's and they stretched out on the hayrack, their bodies pressing together.

Gabby wiped sweat from his brow as he wondered if Kevin and Meredith had opted for alfresco lovemaking to escape the heat of the camper. Or perhaps they'd come outside to afford Jack and Teal privacy, and that thought summoned new images, images quickly erased as Kevin and Meredith tugged at each other's shorts and then tossed them aside with their shirts.

Completely naked now, Kevin looked even skinnier, with narrow shoulders and sunken chest and spindly legs. Meredith's nakedness, on the other hand, revealed pleasing womanly curves where clothing had suggested only roundness. One was a body of boney angles, and the other was softly pliant—so different—yet when he mounted her and her legs wrapped around him, it seemed the most natural of unions.

Still, Gabby watched, his own lust and envy and shame growing as the lovers on the hayrack neared climax, then, as if finding climax himself, he imagined Gwen Todd's lips against his cheek, her breast brushing his arm. He closed his eyes as Meredith sounded a low audible gasp across the yard. Shyness had never been so painful.

CHAPTER 14

▼

It was ten o'clock in the morning, and although Gwen Todd had been working on her monthly report to the city council for over an hour, she'd written only one paragraph. She stared at her computer screen, rereading that paragraph, then she shook her head and hit the delete key. Now, facing a blank screen once more, she placed her hands on the keyboard to begin anew, but words wouldn't come. *This is ridiculous,* she thought. It's not literature. Or poetry. It's a report to the city council, for God's sake. They don't even read the damn things—she was certain of that—but still, the usual pabulum she produced in ten minutes each month wouldn't come, and her thoughts wandered, as they had repeatedly wandered all morning, to the night before.

Something about the night before troubled her, something she couldn't quite put her finger on. She just had a vague, uneasy feeling that now kept her from communicating mundane thoughts to the city council. What was it? She'd had a few beers and smoked some pot. Big deal. It'd been several years since she'd smoked pot, but a few tokes at a private party hardly seemed like a crime spree—especially so, considering that she knew the mayor herself enjoyed a private toke from time to time.

And the Shriners weren't the root of her uneasiness. If anything, she'd found them amusing, with their earnest but callow grasping for the spiritual. They were just kids, after all, with plenty to learn, but they certainly were not a threat to anyone. Nor was Slade Walters a threat. Slade was an ignorant ass, to be sure, and he might spread rumors, but Gwen was confident that nothing would come of it, that her standing in the community was safe from the likes of him. She only hoped that Slade didn't cause trouble for Gabby.

She put her hands to the keyboard again and typed "The library," and then she paused as she realized what was troubling her about the night before. It was Gabby Cox. More precisely, it was their friendship—a friendship that had always played out here in the library and had always been marked by the library's polite and respectful decorum. Now, in the wake of the Sphinx business, their friendship had gone afield to Gabby's farm, where it had taken on a different feel. It was silly, she thought; friendship shouldn't be affected by place. But there was no denying that Gabby Cox in the library and Gabby Cox on the farm were two different men. And now she worried that she'd somehow encouraged the change. She thought back to her leave-taking the night before. She'd been a little high on beer and pot, and Gabby had been so dear, worrying that Slade had shocked and offended her. Her kiss had been the kiss of one friend reassuring another, nothing more, but now in the sober light of day, she worried that Gabby might've put a different meaning on it.

"Knock, knock."

It wasn't the actual sound of knuckles on wood, but rather a man's voice speaking the words. Gwen looked up. He stood in the open doorway to her office, leaning casually against the doorframe. He wore khakis and a dark blue polo shirt, and a camera hung by a strap from his neck. He held a notebook in his hand. His brown hair was neither long nor short, just shaggy, and his mouth seemed on the verge of a sneer, as if prepared for something wretched. It was the facial feature, the almost-sneer, that struck Gwen first, and then she noticed his eyes. A hint of smile played there, at the corners of his eyes, a contrast to his mouth, suggesting there might be humor to go with the wretchedness.

"May I help you?" she asked.

"I truly hope so." He stepped into the office and tossed a business card on her desk. "Tanner Mills. *Star Tribune*."

Gwen studied the card briefly, recognizing the name. "You're a political reporter."

"Ah, my reputation precedes me."

She shrugged. "I read the paper."

"Of course, you do." He flopped uninvited into the chair opposite Gwen. "The library lady's gotta set a good example for the unread, after all."

Gwen hesitated. Tanner Mills seemed pushy, which was to be expected from the media, she supposed, but still, she didn't care for the way he'd barged into her office. "How may I help you, Mr. Mills?"

"Call me Tanner. Or Mills. But skip the mister thing. It gets in the way of honest communication."

I don't think I like you, thought Gwen. "Very well…Mills, what brings you to Hayesboro?"

"The Sphinx thing, of course."

"Hasn't that been reported enough already?"

"I'm gonna do a feature."

"But you're a political reporter. You cover the capitol and the governor's office, don't you?"

He seemed to wince at her question, and the smile briefly left his eyes but then returned. "I'm on special assignment. So far, Sphinx's just been news. Now it's time for the truth. I'm good at getting at the truth."

Gwen was sure now. She didn't like him. "And the news isn't true?"

He shrugged. "Sometimes it is. Sometimes it isn't. Mostly it's just in a hurry."

"And…you're not in a hurry?"

He shrugged again. "I hurry when I have to, though it doesn't look like anything hurries out here in the sticks."

She eyed him a moment. "Are you intentionally trying to make a bad impression, Mr. Mills, or is this just the way one gets at the truth?"

The smile left his eyes again, and when it returned, it included his mouth, changing his expression from cynical to boyish. "Sorry, library lady. Didn't mean to knock your town. Can we start over?"

Now Gwen shrugged, her guard momentarily distracted by his smile.

"I don't mean to be a hard ass," he said. "That comes from too much time at the capitol, I guess. I forgot my library manners."

"Which begs the question, what do you expect to find at the library? I'd think a reporter would start at the sheriff's office. Or at the local newspaper."

He shook his head. "I don't like sheriffs, and they don't like me. And the local paper is competition."

Gwen raised her eyebrows. "The Hayesboro *Gazette*? Competition for the mighty *Star Tribune*?"

"They're still a newspaper. They think like a newspaper. I want a different slant. Besides, I always start at the library. Always have. It's what my mother told me to do." His smile widened into a broad grin.

Gwen eyed him again. She didn't like the boyish Tanner Mills any more than she had liked the cynical one, and she trusted the boyish one less. She felt patronized. She felt pushed. "So Mommy sent you to the library, and there you discovered H. L. Mencken, and you decided to become a journalist, a seeker of truth; is that your story?"

"Funny you should mention Mencken. He's my hero, but actually, no, journalism came later. I was gonna be a biologist."

"That's quite a leap. Biology to journalism."

"Not really. They both involve turning over rocks and looking for the crawly things that hide from the light of day."

Gwen couldn't help a smile at the thought of a young Tanner Mills terrorizing the neighborhood fauna. "So, Mr. Mills, you've come to Hayesboro, and the first rock you've overturned is my library. Found anything crawly?"

He laughed. "No, ma'am. Just one very smart library lady, who I wish would call me Tanner. And while we're talking names, I'd just as soon call you something besides library lady."

She hesitated. "Gwen Todd."

He nodded and wrote her name in his notebook. "Now then, Gwen Todd, in a hundred words or less, please describe the socioeconomic and cultural impact of rock stars falling from the sky onto small Midwestern towns. Feel free to include any relevant anecdotes that lend humanity and grace. That's what we feature writers always look for, humanity and grace."

Gwen couldn't help another smile as she shook her head. "Look, Mr....look, Tanner, I'm really busy. I have a report to finish and—"

"Fine. What're you doing later?"

"Later? How much later?"

He shrugged. "Five o'clock? I assume they've got bars in this burg."

"You want me to have a drink with you?"

"Sure, why not? Then maybe we can grab a bite to eat somewhere."

She felt pushed again. "Look, Mr. Mills, I—"

"Tanner."

"No." She shook her head. "No, I'm sticking with Mr. Mills for now because this is starting to sound like a date, and it's all moving a bit too fast for me."

He held his hands up in mock horror. "A date? I'm not talking about a date."

She eyed him suspiciously. "Well, what else would you call meeting for a drink and dinner?"

The boyish grin returned. "Business."

"How so?"

"Hey, it's a natural business relationship. We're both in the business of disseminating information, right? And you're busy now, so I'm accommodating your schedule by arranging to meet you later. And we gotta eat, right? No, I'm not talking about a date. I'm just suggesting that we be...what? Efficient? Yeah, that's it, efficient. I'm asking you out on an efficiency."

Gwen chuckled in spite of her best effort not to. "You're full of it."

He shrugged. "I suppose, but hey, I got off on the wrong foot. I got pushy, and I shoulda known better. My mother always said, 'Don't be pushy; be polite.' Then I knocked your town. I'm sorry, okay? Besides, I hate eating alone, and I really do think you can help me background this story, so won't you give me a second chance?"

She shook her head, now convinced that he was full of it, but then she surprised herself by saying, "Alright."

He seemed surprised too. "You will?"

She nodded. "Strictly in the interest of the efficient dissemination of information."

"You got it, Gwen Todd. Five o'clock work?"

She nodded again.

"I'll pick you up here at the library. Do I need to dress up for Hayesboro nightlife?"

She shook her head.

"Good, 'cause this is as dressed up as I get."

Then he was gone, leaving Gwen to her city council report, but now different thoughts kept her monthly pabulum from coming. She wondered what could have possibly moved her to agree to go out with him? It wasn't charm; she was sure of that. Tanner Mills wasn't a charming man. If anything, he was arrogant, and Gwen didn't like arrogant men. They reminded her of California.

CHAPTER 15

▼

Nothing in Ron Chrome's demeanor, not his narrowed eyes or the set of his jaw, suggested anything good as he flipped through the file on his desk. He hadn't uttered a word in several minutes, and Gwen Todd's uneasiness grew with his silence. She was sitting across from him, and the file on his desk was Seth Rawlings' résumé, though calling it a résumé was generous. It contained a single coversheet stating Seth's vital statistics. Another sheet listed his bit parts. It was a short list, and only one part had been a speaking part, and that part had only required Seth to say, "Hey!" The rest of the file consisted of glossies, most of which featured him in swim trunks at the beach. The glossies didn't lie. They showed Seth as he was: a handsome hunk, the sort to be found every hundred yards or so on the beach at Malibu, but comparing the file with the résumés of the pictured stars smiling down from Chrome's office walls was pure folly.

Now as the silence stretched to another minute, Gwen's stomach tightened into a knot. Chrome had given Seth's written matter only a cursory glance before tossing it aside, and now he was flipping through the glossies for the fourth time. Gwen had given up hope for anything positive after the second flip-through, concluding that her boss was just killing time while he contemplated her punishment. And she knew better too. She knew that asking Chrome to look at the résumé was a mistake, but she'd promised Seth, so she'd gone ahead, hoping that Chrome would dismiss the whole thing with a roll of his eyes and a gentle admonition not to bother him with this sort of thing again. Now she actually feared for her job—a justifiable risk were she in love with Seth, but she wasn't.

Chrome closed the file and looked up, allowing the silence to continue for a long uncomfortable moment. "Not the sort of résumé we normally look at around here, Toddy."

"I know, and I'm sorry. This was a mistake and—"

"This guy…" Chrome glanced at the coversheet. "This guy, Rawlings, he a friend of yours?"

Gwen nodded.

"You living together, by any chance?"

The question frightened Gwen. It was a dark turn that seemed certain to lead to her firing. "He's sharing my apartment…just now."

"Just now?"

She shrugged. "There aren't any permanent plans. And I don't expect any, either."

He thought for a moment and then nodded. "Okay, bring him in tomorrow. I'll talk to him."

Gwen was shocked. "Are…are you sure? I mean, you said yourself, Ron, this isn't the sort of client we take on. If you're not—"

"Look, Toddy, you brought him up. You want me to talk to him or not?"

Suddenly, Gwen wasn't sure, but her relief at not being fired outweighed her doubt. "Sure."

When Seth heard the news that night, he was ecstatic. His career was finally launched. Surely, stardom was just ahead. He barely slept, such was his excitement, and even his morning run and push-ups failed to calm him. He couldn't eat breakfast, either, something Gwen took as a warning flag. Health-conscious Seth never skipped breakfast, and she also knew that he had to be calm just to be marginally articulate; he babbled when excited. They made love in lieu of breakfast, but instead of calming him, it gave new edge to his excitement, and as they left for the office, Gwen once more feared for her job, thinking she might be fired yet.

The meeting started badly, then got worse. Gwen had hoped to skip it, but Chrome insisted that she sit in. He got right to business. "What's your goal in life, Rawlings?"

Seth flashed a grin, revealing teeth that dazzled white in his tanned face. "I wanna be a star."

Not the noblest ambition, thought Gwen, *but at least to the point.*

"What kinda star?" pressed Chrome.

A harder question. Seth's eyebrows knitted. "A movie star?"

"And what single quality most qualifies you to be a movie star?"

Seth grinned again. He was back on confident ground. "I'm in pretty good shape. And I don't break many mirrors."

Chrome eyed him for a moment. "What sorta roles you see yourself in?"

Seth shrugged. "Leading ones? Maybe ones with a lotta action?"

"Your answers sound like questions. Aren't you sure?"

Seth shrugged again. "Sure I'm sure."

"Tell me about your formal training. Had any acting classes?"

"A few." Seth started to elaborate, but then he blathered about running and push-ups instead.

Several moments passed as Chrome eyed him again. "Why should the Chrome Agency take you on as a client?"

More running and push-up blather.

Chrome glanced at Gwen. *Here it comes*, she thought. *I'm about to be fired.*

Chrome looked back at Seth, his eyes narrowed, allowing the silence to grow uncomfortable, and then he leaned forward. "Okay, Rawlings, here's the deal. You're not ready. Nowhere near ready. There's no way I can offer you a standard Chrome contract."

Seth shrank visibly in his chair.

"But here's what I will do. I'll sign you to a personal services contract."

Seth's face was a mix of confusion and hope. Gwen was just confused. She'd never heard of a personal services contract.

"What's…a personal services contract?" asked Seth.

"Just what it says," said Chrome. "It doesn't involve representing you to the industry. Like I said, you're not ready for that. What it does do is obligate you to perform certain services for the agency, services to be determined by me."

Seth looked wary now. "What…kinda services?"

Chrome shrugged. "Nothing you can't handle. At times, it'll just be errands. Gofer stuff. Other times, you might be helping with some of our PR projects, which'll also give you some exposure. And Rawlings, if you need anything, it's exposure."

"So…do I get paid?"

Chrome nodded. "Say, five hundred bucks a week."

Seth was still wary, but now he looked interested too, and Gwen understood why. She knew that he hadn't earned five hundred dollars in any recent month, much less in a week. Seth thought a moment and then asked, "So, could this personal service thing maybe lead to a regular contract?"

Chrome smiled. "You never know."

Seth glanced at Gwen and then looked back to Chrome, and his face broke into a dazzling grin once more. "Mr. Chrome, you got yourself a deal."

That afternoon, Gwen was called into Chrome's office again. Chrome was reading the *Wall Street Journal,* and he seemed not to notice her. She sat in the chair opposite him, and after a moment, she said, "You wanted to see me?"

He took another moment before folding the paper and facing her. "Yeah, Toddy, I wanna flesh out this Rawlings deal. I need you involved in it."

"Actually, I'm a little confused," she said. "This personal service contract business is new to me. I didn't know we did that sort of thing."

"We don't usually, but from to time, the situation calls for it."

Situation? Gwen wondered what situation could call for giving Seth any kind of contract, and a sense of uneasiness was added to her confusion. "Just what sort of services will Seth be providing?"

"I told you. Errands. PR stuff."

"What kind of PR?"

Chrome leveled his gaze at her. "Tess needs a new boyfriend."

Gwen's eyes widened. "Tess Snow?"

Chrome nodded.

"Ron, Tess needs another boyfriend like she needs…like she needs screwing lessons."

"There, Toddy, you hit the nail on the head. That's Tess's problem. She's too busy screwing everything that walks through the door, and that's keeping her from getting the kind of legit PR she needs."

Gwen shook her head. "I'm totally confused."

"Well, just listen, and you won't be. For one thing, and despite our best efforts to avoid it, there's too much talk around town about Tess going down for anything in pants. And an occasional skirt too."

Gwen shrugged. Nothing new there.

"And I'm not saying she's gotta be a Girl Scout," Chrome continued. "Girl Scouts don't sell any better than sluts. The public *wants* their stars horny and fucking around—that's part of the mystique. They even go for a little lesbo action, but there's a limit to anything, and Tess has crossed the line."

Gwen shrugged again. "I understand all that. I just don't see how Seth fits in."

"You will. There're a number of things I like about your boy. I think he might be the answer to our Tess problem, and you bringing him in just now is perfect timing. There may be a bonus in this for you."

Gwen's stomach knotted again, but now for a different reason. She'd gone from fearing the loss of her job to just fearing her job. "So…what do you like about Seth?"

Chrome held up one finger. "First, he's got the right look. Beach boy is clean-cut, but still sexy. And it's a perfect fit for Tess's next movie, the stranded-on-the-desert-isle bit. We get Tess and Rawlings together with some sun and sand, and we can shine up her image and promo her next movie at the same time. Makes sense, right?"

Gwen nodded after a moment.

Chrome held up two fingers. "Second, Rawlings comes cheap. We still gotta watch the bottom line around here. And I don't think he's all that smart, either. That's a plus too. It's easier to control guys who do what they're told and don't think too much."

Gwen felt a stab of shame. Seth might not be the brightest guy on the block, but that didn't give the agency license to use him like this. And Seth had only agreed because of Chrome's vague suggestion that it might lead to a standard contract. Gwen knew that would never happen, and it made the whole thing all the more shameful.

Chrome held up a third finger. "Last—and here's where you come in, Toddy—I like that he lives with you. That maximizes control, see, and since you've got no long-term plans for him, you can be professional and do what's best for the agency. You're in the perfect position to work him."

Gwen said nothing as she contemplated the meaning of professional.

Chrome studied her for a moment. "That's right, isn't it, Toddy? You don't have a thing for Rawlings, do you?"

"No. We're sharing an apartment, that's all. We're just friends."

"Friends is fine. And sleeping together's not a problem, either. It's not like he's a client."

Gwen felt her face redden. "We're just friends, Ron."

Chrome nodded. "Good."

"But I still don't see what you hope to accomplish. How does a phony relationship with Seth and some PR shots on the beach clean up Tess's image? How'll that keep her from screwing everything that walks through the door?"

Chrome smiled. "That won't matter anymore, Toddy. See, our problem's been that we haven't put out our own message. We left it to Tess, and that was a mistake. And it was my mistake; I'll take the blame. But now we're gonna do it right. We're gonna get our own message out there. That's the name of the game, Toddy. Manage the message. You manage the message right, and all of a sudden, it doesn't matter what Tess does. Manage the message, and the truth can't hurt you. Manage the message, and the public'll think it is the truth."

Gwen sighed. "It seems awfully…complicated."

"You don't worry about the complications, Toddy. I'll tend to the nuances. You just tend to Rawlings, okay?"

Gwen nodded. She felt like a pimp.

CHAPTER 16

▼

Gabby stepped from the kitchen onto the porch and froze at the sight of an airplane diving toward his barn. In the next instant, he realized that there were three airplanes, and it took yet another instant for him to realize that it was a kite. The kite, made to depict three jets in tight formation, pulled out of its dive at the last moment to soar high above the charred ruins once more. The kite's flight was accompanied by Sphinx's now familiar signature song, booming across the barnyard.

Baby, baby, come ride my cloud,
We'll slip the Earth and fly so proud.

The kite reached maximum height and looped earthward. Gabby followed its path, down, down, until his gaze came upon Jack Sand, working the kite string in the middle of the yard. Standing a few feet away, Teal Osborne and Kevin Calm and Meredith Towne were waving their arms rhythmically in the air and singing along with the boom box. It was all playful enough, but to Gabby it also had the feel of a ceremony or rite.

Once more, the jets pulled out of their dive at the last moment to soar skyward again.

So spread your legs on this cloud so soft,
Higher and higher and higher

The jets reached their apex and looped downward. Jack worked the string. Too late. The jets smashed into a blackened timber that had once supported the barn's hayloft. The string went slack, and the three-jet formation hung in a tangle of torn plastic. Teal, Kevin, and Meredith lowered their arms.

And I'll fill you as we soar aloft.

Kevin reached down and turned off the boom box, and the Shriners dropped to their knees, as if on cue, and bowed their heads.

Now it seemed even more like a ceremony to Gabby, one that held an unwelcome twinge of déjà vu. He didn't care to be reminded of aircraft crashing into his barn, but the Shriners' solemn pose seemed to demand quiet respect for the moment. Then the quiet was broken by the sound of a car driving into the yard. Gabby turned to look. It was the sheriff's cruiser, and Sam Stack was at the wheel. For Gabby it was another twinge of déjà vu: Sam being the first to arrive after a plane crash.

Sam parked near the house and climbed from the car and stood eyeing the Shriners. The Shriners were still on their knees and were casting wary glances at the sheriff. This guarded mutual appraisal continued as Gabby walked up to the car.

"What's up, Sam?"

Sam eyed the Shriners a moment longer and then turned. "There's a rumor going around town that troubles me a bit, Gabby. Thought I'd better check it out."

"What sorta rumor?"

Sam glanced at the Shriners again. "That you got some kinda hippie commune going out here."

"Sam, this ain't the seventies. I reckon hippies've gone the way of beatniks."

Sam looked surprised. "What the hell you know about beatniks?"

Gabby shrugged. "I read. I go to the library."

"Well, whatever you call 'em, folks are talking."

"Let 'em talk. There ain't no law against parking a camper in a barnyard, Sam."

Sam eyed him for a moment. "Well, Slade Walters says there's a lot more going on out here than camping. Says there're drugs out here. Says there're people smoking marijuana."

"I figure Slade's been misinformed."

"Says he saw it himself, Gabby. Says he was out here last night and that he saw a bunch of hippies smoking marijuana and that the hippies jumped him. About ten of 'em, he figured. Says he hadda fight his way outta here."

"Ten, huh?" Gabby snorted. "Sam, you ain't gonna find one hippie out here, much less ten."

Sam nodded toward the Shriners. "Who are they?"

"Sphinx fans. They drove all the way from New York just to see where the plane crashed. They're just fans, Sam. They ain't hurting nothing. I gave 'em permission to camp a few days, and that's all there is to it."

Sam watched as the Shriners slowly shuffled to their camper and then went out of sight behind it. "Sphinx fans, huh? They look kinda nervous with me around. Why's that?"

"They're spiritual," Gabby explained.

"Spiritual? What's that got to do with anything?"

Gabby shrugged. "I reckon spiritual folks are less likely to give you trouble."

Sam snorted. "Don't bet on it. And while were on the subject of trouble, Slade does have a pretty nasty bruise on his forehead."

"Who knows what he might've bumped into? He was pretty drunk."

"So then, he was out here last night."

Gabby hesitated and then tried to change the subject. "Any word from the feds yet?"

"About what?"

"About Sphinx. About what he was doing out here and about why he crashed?"

Sam shook his head. "I reckon he crashed because he hit your cottonwood tree over yonder, but that's way too simple an explanation for the feds. They'll mull it over for weeks, maybe months, and when they do release their findings, you'll have to look damn hard to find the word 'tree' in any of it. One thing's for sure: they'll find that he was high on something, but as to what he was doing out here, we may never know that. But don't go changing the subject on me, Gabby. We're talking about Slade Walters and marijuana. Now, suppose you give me your side of it."

Sam's persistent questions made Gabby feel like a criminal. He didn't like it, especially not on his own land. "We were having a barbecue, that's all, and Slade came along, drunk as usual, and made an ass of himself."

"Was Gwen Todd here too?"

Anger flashed across Gabby's face. "What's Slade saying about her?"

"That she was here, partying with the hippies."

"Goddamn it, Sam, there ain't any hippies. And Gwen had been out seeing her dad, and she dropped off some sweet corn because I'd asked her to, and then she stayed for supper. That's all there was to it."

"And no one smoked marijuana?"

Gabby looked down at his feet. "I've never used the stuff in my life. Not once, and that's the truth. Besides, what goes on out here is nobody's business but mine."

"Goddamn it, Gabby, I didn't ask if you were smoking the stuff. I asked if anyone was. And don't give me that it's-my-land-and-I'll-do-what-I-want crap. I'm doing you a favor here. I'm trying to head this thing off before it gets outta hand."

"What's to head off? You figure folks'll believe Slade over me?"

"That's not the point, Gabby. Rumors got a way of growing legs and walking around on their own. Sure, people take Slade with a grain of salt, but you don't wanna let it get beyond Slade. You don't want, say, Hester Cronk getting into this."

Gabby frowned. "Hester? How'd this be any of her business?"

Sam shrugged. "You know Hester. If she decides something's her business, then it's her business. And it's an election year, Gabby. A hippie commune is just the sorta issue she'll sink her teeth into. She'll always take a good crusade over dull stuff like taxes and budgets, stuff she doesn't understand anyway."

"I told you, Sam, they ain't hippies and there wasn't any marijuana. They're just Sphinx fans, and that's all there is to it."

"*Spiritual* Sphinx fans. That was your own word, Gabby—spiritual—and I suspect it'll be a red flag if Hester hears it."

"No reason for her to hear it, Sam. Unless you tell her. I sure ain't gonna."

Sam shook his head and sighed. "Look, Gabby, I'm not trying to pick a fight with you. All I'm saying is that it'd probably be a good idea for your…campers to move on, and to do it soon."

"You telling me who I can have as guests on my own land?"

"No, Gabby, I'd never tell you that. And don't get constitutional with me. I'm trying to help. Just be careful, okay?"

Gabby shrugged.

Sam stared at him for a moment and then shook his head again and climbed into the car. He started the engine and looked out the side window at Gabby as if to say something, but he changed his mind and drove off instead, muttering, "Goddamn bachelor farmers," to himself.

CHAPTER 17

▼

"So this is nightlife in Hayseed?" Tanner Mills' tone was heavy with sarcasm, and his upper lip curled in his usual sneer as he looked about the darkened interior of Ted's Tavern.

They were seated in a booth, and Gwen Todd wondered if choosing Ted's had been a mistake. It certainly wasn't the fanciest place in town. It was a roadhouse at the edge of Hayesboro, a smoky bar that also served greasy burgers. It'd seemed a good choice because it was dark and private—for reasons she didn't fully understand, she wanted to avoid being seen with Tanner in a very public place—but now she had to admit that Ted's, in addition to being dark and private, was also seedy. Their booth seats were wooden and hard, and more than a few initials were carved in the tabletop. Much of the dim lighting served the dual purpose of advertising beer, and most of the caps worn by the men lining the bar advertised agricultural products. She felt an urge to apologize for it all, and that angered her. It also angered her that Tanner had just called the town Hayseed for the third time.

She sipped her white wine and then summoned her iciest tone. "On behalf of everyone in...*Hayseed*, I apologize that we aren't up to your usual standards."

His sneer disappeared. "Sorry. I'm getting off on the wrong foot again, aren't I?"

"You seem to have a knack."

He sipped his beer. "Sorry," he apologized again. "Truth be told, I'm not all that happy about this assignment, but I shouldn't take it out on your town. That's not very generous of me."

"So why aren't you happy? I thought you were all hot to do your Sphinx feature."

"The Sphinx thing's my editor's idea. I got in the governor's doghouse over a thing I wrote about his son and a St. Paul whorehouse…"

"I remember reading that."

"…and my editor decided that I hadda get outta Dodge for a while. Ergo, here I am in Haysee…Hayesboro."

Gwen shrugged. "I should think a reporter, a professional one anyway, would be happy to go wherever the story is and do the job."

"Ouch! That's cutting a little close to the bone, library lady. And you're right, of course. I'm not acting very professionally, but in my defense, I submit that it's not much fun being in the governor's doghouse."

"That is *so* tragic."

He ignored her sarcasm. "And on top of that, my girlfriend dumped me, so you can see that I've got plenty of reasons to feel sorry for myself."

Gwen was quite certain that she didn't want to discuss Tanner's girlfriend troubles. "You poor dear. Actually, it sounds as if a nice rest in the countryside is just what you need."

He smiled ruefully. "Trouble is, I don't find the countryside all that restful. In fact, it makes me nervous. I feel scrutinized. I miss the anonymity of the city."

She chuckled. "That's rather ironic from someone who makes a living scrutinizing things."

He shrugged. "I guess it makes a difference whether you're the scrutinizer or the scrutinizee."

She chuckled again, and they both sipped their drinks. Then he added, "And while I'm confessing things, it should be noted that I came to Hayesboro with a preconceived bias against the place."

"How's that?"

"Your illustrious state senator."

"Hester Cronk?"

He nodded. "She's not one of my favorites in the legislature, and since you people keep sending her back, it sorta colors my view."

Senator Cronk wasn't a favorite of Gwen's, either, but she didn't say as much. "For someone who's supposed to be an objective journalist, you've got all sorts of biases: first, it's small towns, and now it's Republicans."

"Oh, it's not a party thing. I treat Republicans and Democrats with equal disdain, but with Hester it's different. She may sport a Republican label, but she actually caucuses with God."

Gwen smiled and sipped her wine.

Tanner raised his beer mug to his lips and then lowered it. "Maybe I'm outta line again. Maybe Hester's your favorite politician. For all I know, you might've run her last campaign."

Gwen laughed and shook her head. "No, Tanner, when it comes to Hester Cronk, you and I are in total agreement. She's a bit pious for my tastes."

"Good. That's how I had you figured. You don't seem the Hester type, but you never know with these small towns."

"There you go, bashing small towns again. Can't someone live in a small town and still be thoughtful and discerning?"

"C'mon, library lady. Sure, you're thoughtful and discerning, but you didn't get that way here at Ted's Tavern. Where'd you go to school?"

"The University of Minnesota."

"Aha! I studied a little hedonism there myself. But what I don't get is how someone can go to an eye-opening place like that and then come back here to Hayseed."

She glared at him.

"Sorry, Hayesboro."

"Well, Tanner, it's not as if I'm the only college grad in town."

"Yeah, but after the 'U,' didn't you have an urge to get out and see the world?"

"I did work in L.A. for a while. In Hollywood, actually."

"Whoa! You did Tinsel Town?"

"Does that qualify as seeing the world?"

"Well, if you wanna know the truth, I didn't have you figured for that type. But that makes it even more a case of how-you-gonna-keep-em-down-on-the-farm. How does someone go from Hollywood to Hayesboro?"

She sipped her wine. "It's a long story."

"So? I got all night."

No you don't, she thought, *not with me anyway.* "Actually, I have an early meeting tomorrow, so we should think about eating. The burgers here at Ted's are decent, or there're a couple other options in town if you want something better, so long as you understand that better is pretty much limited to steak or shrimp. That's the extent of haute cuisine in Hayesboro."

Tanner pressed his palm to his forehead in mock concentration. "My God! So many choices! Maybe we oughta have another round and discuss it. And why the rush? I'm just a lonely reporter in town with nowhere else to go, and we've got a lot to talk about."

She raised an eyebrow. "Like the lonely reporter's girlfriend?"

"Ex-girlfriend! Geez, I knew it was a mistake the second after I mentioned her, but really, she's history." He smiled. "She ran off with a motorcycle gang."

Gwen laughed. "I don't believe you."

"It's true. She's got ten tattoos, D-cup implants, and a mustache, but I don't wanna talk about her. I wanna talk about you in Tinsel Town."

Before Gwen could respond, a new presence loomed next to their booth. "Well, look who's out partying again tonight."

Gwen knew it was Slade Walters without looking up. When she did look up, he was standing there with a beer in his hand and a smirk on his face. The dim light did nothing to conceal his shaggy beard or his beer gut or, for that matter, the large bruise on his forehead.

His voice slurred when he spoke again. "What'll folks say 'bout the town librarian running with strange men every night?"

Tanner looked up at Slade. "We're having a private conversation here, pal. Why don't you just move along?"

Slade turned his smirk on Tanner. "I don't know who the fuck you are, but you ain't no pal of mine."

Gwen, suddenly horrified at the prospect of being entangled in Slade's rowdiness on consecutive nights, spoke with all the authority she could muster. "That's enough, Slade. Move along."

Slade ignored her, focusing on Tanner. "You from the commune out at the Cox place? Don't recognize you, but I 'spose there's new ones coming every day." He jabbed a finger in Tanner's face. "You best be careful— that's all I got to say. Folks are watching. We know what's going on out there."

"I mean it, Slade." Gwen's voice rose, and heads turned at the bar. "Leave or I'll call the manager."

Slade snorted. "The manager, huh? Where the hell you think you are? The goddamn library? This is Ted's, lady."

Tanner slid to the edge of the booth, but Gwen held up her hand. "Don't, Tanner. He's not worth it."

Slade sneered at her and then turned to Tanner. "That's right, *pal.* You know what's good for you, you'll stay in that booth. And remember what I told you. We're watching." He glared a moment longer before he finally turned and lumbered off.

Tanner watched him go and then let out a long breath. "Now that's what I call thoughtful and discerning."

Gwen shook her head. "Would you believe that in his rare sober moments he's a pilot? A crop duster?"

Disbelief registered on Tanner's face. "They let *that* fly an airplane?"

Gwen nodded.

"Amazing." Tanner looked up after thinking for a moment. "What's this business about a commune?"

"It's nothing."

"He mentioned the Cox place. That's where Sphinx crashed, isn't it? Is there a commune out there? Now that'd be an interesting coincidence. Just the sort of thing that might turn a dull feature into an interesting one."

"There's no commune, Tanner," Gwen said, now wary of the reporter stirring in him. "Where do you want to eat?"

He thought a moment. "You decide. Right after we have another round."

CHAPTER 18

▼

"Thank you, Mr. Beard. I'm so glad you called. I'm quite certain that God is speaking to me through you."

Howard Cronk was trying to watch the Minnesota Twins on TV, but the words his wife had just spoken into the phone rasped at his attention like a nail on a blackboard. Over the years, he'd grown wary of Hester's communications from God. It didn't happen often. A year or two might pass between heavenly ordainments, but when God did speak to Hester, it usually complicated Howard's life.

The first time, at least the first time in Howard's experience, had occurred twenty-four years earlier. He was in the army, stationed at Fort Sill, and he was in a bar in Lawton, Oklahoma, with his buddy, Larry. They each had a forty-eight-hour pass and the hope of getting laid, and if that hope went unfulfilled, their fallback plan was to get drunk. They were now on their third beer each, and the ratio of soldiers to girls in the bar was about 50 to 1; hope was waning.

It shouldn't be this hard, thought Howard. He was darkly handsome, and the army had added to his shoulders and subtracted from his waist, and all that was nicely presented in a well-fitted uniform. So where was a girl to appreciate it? It'd always come easy back home in Minnesota, but then, Minnesota wasn't overrun by the army. Goddamn army. Goddamn Oklahoma. He drained his mug, reconciling himself to the fallback plan, and he was reaching into his pocket for beer money when Larry walked up to their table with a girl on each arm.

Hot damn, thought Howard. Student nurses! Good old Larry had really come through. Student nurses were the wildest dream of every poor bastard living in a Fort Sill barracks, and it looked as if Larry had already picked his out. She was the shorter of the two, and her tight black skirt showed off her ass as nicely as her tight red sweater showed off her breasts. She was smiling up at Larry and rubbing those nice breasts against his right arm, leaving no doubt that the left-arm girl was Howard's.

The left-arm girl didn't stretch her clothes as much as the right arm girl, and Howard also saw that she was the prettier of the two, but then Larry wasn't paying much attention to faces. Introductions were made. The left-arm girl was named Hester McBride. She smiled sweetly at Howard and released Larry's arm. Howard's hopes soared and then plummeted a moment later at the news that the girls weren't student nurses at all. They were from the nearby Bible college.

Jesus, Larry! Bible college students? The night was lost. There was no hope of getting laid now, and to make matters worse, these girls would probably throw cold water on the fallback plan. For some reason, though, Larry was flushed with confidence. Probably the beer, thought Howard, but then they all sat down and got a pitcher of beer, and Larry's girl kept rubbing her boobs against his arm, and Hester kept smiling at Howard, and soon, Howard's hopes began inching upward again.

Larry and Boobs left the bar first. Howard and Hester left fifteen minutes later, and it took only another twenty minutes for them to check into a motel room and then just another five minutes to get naked.

She was beautiful. Her body was slender, yet nicely curved, and when she came into his arms, her small breasts felt firm and wonderful against his chest.

Suddenly, she pushed away. "We have to pray first," she said.

"Huh?"

"We have to pray," she repeated, then she knelt at the side of the bed. Howard stood dumbstruck, and after a moment, she commanded, "Kneel down."

Howard knelt beside her.

"Bow your head," she ordered.

Howard did as he was told, though the obeisance of bowing seemed off-set by his erection. He hoped God wasn't offended.

Hester prayed aloud for God's blessing. Howard prayed silently for an end to the praying and a start to the screwing.

His prayer was answered, and afterward, he was startled by the evidence of her virginity on the sheet. "You're...I was the first?"

"Of course."

"Wow," was all Howard could think to say.

"Does that surprise you?"

"Yes. Um...no. I mean, I don't know."

She took his hands and looked steadily into his eyes. "Howard, you must understand that God intended this. He sent you to me. He's speaking to us. This is God's will."

"Um...it is?"

"We have to get married, Howard."

"We do?"

She nodded solemnly. "That's God's will too."

Howard and Hester were married the next week. Six months later, Hester graduated from Bible college, and a month after that, Howard was discharged from the army. Hester had lived her entire life in Oklahoma, but when Howard suggested that they move to Hayesboro, Minnesota, where he could join his family's plumbing and heating business, she agreed immediately. "It's God's will," she explained.

The next ten years were good years, quiet years, a time when Howard worked in the family business and then took it over after his father's death. Hester was content to be a homemaker and keep the books at Cronk Plumbing and Heating. God spoke to her only on rare occasions, such as the births of their son and daughter, and even then only to ordain that their names be Ezekiel and Naomi. Then, as the children grew, Hester became active in their schooling, and suddenly God had much to say again.

Ninth-grade biology at Hayesboro High included a section on Darwinian evolution. It'd been part of the curriculum for years, but that fact had escaped Hester until Ezekiel reached ninth grade. Suddenly, Hester became a regular at Hayesboro School Board meetings, demanding to know why creationism wasn't taught as well. The board did their best to ignore her, which proved a mistake. Hester ran for the school board in the next election, unseating incumbent George Hawkins, the local druggist who had made the mistake of remarking that he could see a family resemblance between monkeys and a few folks in town.

Not coincidentally at all, the board chairman arranged for an official from the state department of education to be on hand for Hester's first board meeting, to explain state curriculum mandates as they applied to the sciences. The official was a confident, hatchet-faced woman with a master's degree who intoned minutiae as well as any of her fellow mandarins back in St. Paul, but she proved no match for Hester. Hester had anticipated the chairman's strategy and packed the meeting with Adam and Eve advocates. Each bureaucratic utterance from the official was countered by a well-chosen Bible verse from Hester and cheers from the crowd. In less than thirty minutes, the department of education official was reduced to helpless blather, and Hester Cronk's political career was launched. A star was born.

Creationism remained a landmark issue for Hester, but the issue she rode into the Minnesota State Senate four years later was gay marriage.

Orlin Peterson was sixty years old and a Lutheran pastor in south Minneapolis. He was a mild-mannered man, guided by the belief that peace and understanding ought to be the chief virtues of Christians, that it was good to contemplate the mysteries of God, but that mortals ought not presume to know them. Orlin also believed that patience is a worthy virtue, but as he grew older, his patience with his fellow Christians grew thin and then finally disappeared.

One day, he returned home from a fractious committee meeting at church and remarked to his wife, Barbara, "Every asshole in the congregation knows God's will better than me." Barbara was shocked, of course, but not nearly as shocked as the congregation when, a week later, Orlin officiated at a marriage ceremony for two gay men. The shock then rippled outward in unceasing and growing waves. The church board threatened dismissal. The bishop threatened defrocking. The Council for Family Values warned of "the certain destruction of the institution of marriage and civilization as we know it." Gay rights groups rallied to the cause, and the storm swirled to an ever-higher pitch. On the day that several thousand gay rights supporters demonstrated on one side of the capitol lawn, while several thousand more, bent on protecting families, lathered on the other side, Hester Cronk filed for the Minnesota State Senate as a Republican.

In announcing her candidacy, Hester noted that God had told her to run. The media pressed for details of the conversation, and Hester responded that God speaks to the heart, that mere ears cannot hear his truth through the din of a sinful world, that only the heart can hear God's true message. "Listen to your heart! Vote for Hester Cronk!" became the catchphrase of Hester's campaign, and an amendment to the state constitution banning gay marriage became her chief issue.

Hamish Duncan was a three-term incumbent in the state senate. He was a lawyer and a middle-of-the-road Democrat with a libertarian streak. He believed in compromise and consensus-building, and true to his Scottish heritage, he was naturally inclined toward reserve and away from bombast. He saw gay marriage as a distraction from the business that government ought to be tending, and when pressed for his stand on the issue, he put it off and talked of budgets instead. He hoped that incumbency would be enough to ward off Hester's onslaught, but he overestimated incumbency and underestimated Hester. By Election Day, he had been painted as an enemy of family values, a spineless politician with no morals. There were even rumors that Hamish himself was gay. Hester won in a landslide.

The Minnesota Twins were trailing by two runs in the bottom of the ninth, but they had men on second and third with two outs. Following a crack of the bat, a single looped into left field, and Howard leaned forward in his chair. One runner scored, and then as the base runner from second rounded third, Hester suddenly appeared, standing in front of the TV.

"There's a satanic cult out at the Cox farm," she said.

Howard craned to see around her. "Out at the plate," said the TV announcer. "Twins lose."

"Goddamn it!" said Howard.

"Howard! Your language! You don't deal with a serious matter like a cult by stooping to profanity."

Howard thought to explain that he'd taken the Lord's name in vain because the Twins had lost, not because of some cult, but then he realized that it wouldn't matter to Hester, so he offered a remorseful shrug instead. Now she stood there, one hand on her hip and a notepad in her other hand, studying the notes she'd taken during her just-completed phone conversation.

She's still a good-looking woman, he thought. She hadn't gained a pound since that night in the Oklahoma bar twenty-four years earlier, and her pretty face belied her years. "Petite" was a word often used to describe her, a word Hester liked, and "ladylike" was acceptable too. She didn't like "feminine" though. It was too close to "feminist."

Howard still passed for handsome too, though it was a middle-aged, jowly handsomeness, and his old army uniform was now several sizes too small. Still, they were an attractive couple, and now that their nest was empty—Ezekiel and Naomi were off to college at Hester's alma mater in Oklahoma—Howard had hopes for rekindled romance, but it wasn't to be. Hester's political career saw to that. She'd chosen the senate over sex, and whenever he complained about all the time she was away, she reminded him that it was God's will. Howard thought that a bit too convenient, that God wouldn't really mind if he got a little nooky now and then, but now God had spoken to Hester again, and Howard was fairly certain that it wasn't about nooky.

"So who was on the phone?" Howard asked.

"An attorney from Minneapolis." Hester consulted her notes. "H. Landon Beard."

"And he says there's a cult out at the Cox place?" This didn't ring right to Howard. Gabby just wasn't the cult type.

"Yes," said Hester, "and they're performing satanic rituals. And none of this comes as a surprise to me. I told you right after that awful Sphinx crashed his plane out there that Satan had a hand in it."

"And those were this Beard guy's actual words? He said satanic cult?"

Hester paused to look at her notes again. "He didn't have to. I've read about these things. I've studied them. What he described is a cult, and there's no doubt in my mind that Satan's behind it."

"So how is this any of Beard's business anyway?"

Hester glared. "Mr. Beard is clearly an upright citizen who's justifiably concerned about today's moral decline. And why shouldn't it be his business? These cults are an affront to God. They're everyone's business."

Howard felt a growing weariness. He knew that when Hester said something was everyone's business, what she really meant was that it was her business, and whatever became Hester's business soon became Howard's business too. The trap was closing, and he stretched to escape it. "So why'd Beard call you?"

"Well, Howard, this is happening in my district, after all. And I do have a reputation in these matters."

"So he just called to let you know? He doesn't want you to do anything?"

"Of course, I'm going to do something. And Mr. Beard will be my ally. He even offered his professional services should a lawyer be needed, which in my view makes him a true Christian soldier."

Howard was now certain of two things: one, he didn't like H. Landon Beard, and two, he would soon be meeting the man.

"We should get the crucifix out," said Hester. "I want it cleaned up and ready."

Howard sighed. Hester used her crucifix when she campaigned. It stood eight feet tall and included a sandy-haired, blue-eyed Jesus with Anglo-Saxon features. Howard thought of it as the Scottish Jesus, but he knew better than to say as much to Hester. It was wrapped in plastic and stored next to some plumbing supplies at the back of the Cronks' oversized garage. Hester usually didn't bring it out until after Labor Day, when the campaign heated up, but now plans had changed. Now there was a satanic cult out at Gabby Cox's farm.

CHAPTER 19

▼

Gwen Todd felt as if she were fifteen again, and Tanner Mills' embrace had much to do with that. They were standing on the flagstone porch at the front of her house, and she hadn't been surprised when he circled his arms around her and kissed her softly on the lips. She was surprised, though, when his hands strayed lower to grope her butt and pull her hips against his as the kiss grew hard.

It'd been a long time—perhaps back to when she was fifteen—since she'd stood outside a door and been surprised by a date's unexpected advance on her butt or breast. Back then, the door had led to the brick house on the Todd farm, and her reaction the first time or two had been to push away and murmur no. She was supposed to slap the boy—that'd been her mother's counsel—but when the time came, slapping seemed extreme, given the compliment of sorts that went with the offense. But now the door she stood outside of didn't lead to the house out on the farm; it lead to her own house in town, and she was no longer fifteen. She was thirty-eight, and Tanner was about the same age, and slapping seemed even less appropriate. She even thought a moment before murmuring no.

Tanner's grope wasn't the first surprise of the night. She'd surprised herself by agreeing to two more rounds of drinks at Ted's Tavern after the Slade Walters episode. She was further surprised at how the drinks and conversation softened Tanner's edge and revealed his humor. They then moved on to dinner at a steakhouse in town, where they lingered long over coffee and easy banter. Now it was nearly midnight, which surprised Gwen too, but what surprised her even more was how much fun she'd had with Tanner, something she'd have given scant chance just hours earlier. Still, she murmured no.

His hands retreated from her butt. "It is kinda public out here. Maybe we oughta go inside."

Hayesboro at midnight was hardly public, she thought. Several hours earlier, the high school band had given their weekly concert in the bandstand across the street in the park, but now all was quiet, save for the crickets chirping in the summer night. No, it wasn't public, but she had no intention of inviting him in, either. "It's late, Tanner, and tomorrow's a work day."

"Dang! Stopped at the goal line! Denied the end zone." His hands slipped down to her butt again.

She couldn't help a giggle. "One more God-awful sports analogy, and you're out for the season."

"Sorry. Hey, out for the season's a sports analogy too. How come you can do it and I can't?"

"Because mine wasn't as awful as yours. And get your hands off my end zone."

His hands moved to the small of her back. "So you don't do it on the first date, huh?"

She leaned back in mock surprise. "Date? Why, Mr. Mills, you assured me this was to be an efficiency when you persuaded me to go out with you, that it'd be strictly about business."

"Well…I happen to favor passionate efficiency."

She shook her head. "Not tonight, Tanner."

"Tomorrow night then?"

"Tanner!"

"Well, we're gonna be together tomorrow anyway. We ought to at least plan on dinner again."

"What makes you think we'll be together tomorrow?"

"Because you said you'd help with my story. And I need you along when I go to see this Cox guy."

"Why?"

"Because he's your friend. Because you can get him to open up." His right hand slid up to caress her left shoulder.

"Gabriel's a very private person. I don't know that I want to help you invade his privacy."

"Hell, his privacy's already invaded. And you said yourself that there's nothing to this commune business. Help me get the story right, and it'll stop the rumors. That's to his benefit."

"Yes, I'm sure Gabriel's benefit is your chief concern here."

"C'mon, Gwen, you've read my stuff. Give me credit for some professionalism. I'm no yellow journalist. I'll treat him right."

She hesitated. "I'm busy all morning tomorrow."

"After lunch then?"

She hesitated again. "Alright, but you'd better do right by Gabriel, or you will be out for the season."

He smiled. "I'll pick you up at the library."

She nodded.

"Then we'll do dinner again tomorrow night."

"Maybe."

His hand slipped from her shoulder to the upper slope of her breast. "And then who knows what else?"

She pushed his hand away. "Good night, Tanner."

*   *   *   *

It was nearly one in the morning when Gwen finally crawled into bed, well past her usual bedtime, but thoughts of Tanner Mills still kept her awake until after two. Yes, he had proven to be both likeable and amusing that evening, but now as she lay there in the dark, she knew it wasn't likeability or amusement that kept sleep away. There was more. His touch had evoked a visceral stirring, and now the memory of his hands on her body was vivid. It had been some time since she'd felt this way, longer than she cared to admit, and because it had happened on her own front porch, it was strangely different too. For reasons Gwen didn't fully understand, she'd always taken pains to keep her sex life, episodic as it was, separate from Hayesboro. Perhaps it was small town nosiness that she sought to avoid, or perhaps it went back to her California days and to things so foreign to her life now, but whatever the reason, her sex life had remained both episodic and out-of-town. There had been John, a fellow librarian from Minneapolis. They met at a conference and became friends and then weekend lovers for a period of five years. Before that, there'd been Stewart, an acquaintance from college who'd moved to Duluth. Stewart meant water: weekend rendezvous along Lake Superior and annual winter trips to the sleepy island of Culebra in the Caribbean. Her water days with Stewart had spanned another five years, and before that there were a few affairs of less duration and intensity, and before that was California.

CHAPTER 20

▼

Seth Rawling's first assignment under his personal service contract with the Chrome Agency was to teach Tess Snow to surf. Tess was agile and lithe, and she was soon riding the waves with grace, which was good considering that a camera was never far away. Being photographed pitching head over heels beneath a crashing breaker just wouldn't be star-like, though Tess did take spill or two. In her most memorable spill, the wave tore loose her bikini top, which required only the parting of a slender string. The camera then shuttered just as Tess stood knee deep in foam with strands of wet blonde hair partially concealing a look of both surprise and pleasure as sunlight gleamed off her wet breasts.

The photo made all the tabloids and movie magazines; Ron Chrome saw to that. "It's perfect, Toddy, absolutely perfect," Chrome raved to Gwen as they toted up Tess's exposure in his office a week later. "You can't buy better PR. You can't create something like this. It just happens, but the beauty here is that we *did* create it. We're managing the message."

Chrome smiled happily at the irony of this, and Gwen nodded her agreement, though she lacked her boss's enthusiasm.

"It's the naturalness, Toddy—that's the key thing. We could've posed Tess topless, but it wouldn't've had half the impact. Hell, there's not a woman in this town that won't bare her boobs for this sorta exposure, but it don't work when you pose it. It's gotta be natural and spontaneous, and the camera knows natural. The camera knows surprise. You can't fool the camera, so we didn't try. We didn't pose Tess. Instead, we put her in a situation where she's doing something natural and athletic and wholesome, and then boom, along comes a wave and bares her boobs for us. It's genius; that's what it is, Toddy."

None of this surprised Gwen, not even the wholesomeness of bare breasts. Ron Chrome had been deftly manipulating public opinion for years. It's what he did best. It was the secret to his success. Nor was Gwen surprised when, after a few surfing lessons, Seth began spending nights at Tess's house. After all, Tess would screw anything, so why wouldn't she screw a hunk like Seth? No, Gwen wasn't surprised, but Seth's new bedmate meant the end of her own affair with him. Her pride dictated that; Seth would not be allowed into her bed on the nights he didn't make it into Tess's. On those nights—two or three times a week—Seth slept on Gwen's couch in the living room, and that close proximity allowed for the close control Ron Chrome wanted to maintain over Seth. And so Gwen ceased being Seth Rawling's lover, about which she was largely indifferent, but she remained his pimp of sorts, about which she was largely troubled.

Seth took their altered relationship and his sleeping on the couch in stride. And why wouldn't he? He was bedding a star and getting his picture in movie magazines. To his way of thinking, he'd arrived, his dream was coming true, and Gwen didn't have the heart to tell him otherwise. She knew that soon enough, Seth's value to Ron Chrome would end. She knew that after Tess's current film, a beach-boy boyfriend would be expendable, and then Seth's bubble-like fantasy would burst, but she saw no reason to hasten his pain. Given a choice between Seth's naïve philandering and Chrome's ruthless manipulation, Gwen's sympathies were with Seth. She still thought of him as a friend, albeit a somewhat clueless friend.

If anything about all this did surprise Gwen, it was how much confidence Seth gained from being used. It was another measure of his naïveté, she supposed, but still, it seemed ironic that being so without guile could lead to such bold assurance. At times he was downright cocky, telling Gwen that he and Tess were destined to be the next Frankie Avalon and Annette Funicello.

Then, after several weeks with his head in the clouds, Seth spent three straight nights on Gwen's couch. He was moody and quiet and began repeating his morning run and push-ups in the afternoon—a sure sign of stress. Gwen was increasingly curious, and when Seth appeared at her Venice apartment for the forth night in a row, she pried, wondering if something was happening contrary to agency design.

"Are you and Tess fighting or something?" she asked.

"Naw," said Seth, avoiding eye contact.

"Weren't you supposed to be with her at the beach this afternoon?"

"Yeah. Surf was lousy, though. She left right away."

Gwen's sense that all was not right with Frankie and Annette grew stronger. "Seth, if there's a problem here, you ought to tell me about it."

He made eye contact now. His look was curious. "Why?"

"Well…because Ron'll want to know. This isn't just about you and Tess. The agency's got an interest here too." She felt like a pimp again.

Seth shrugged. "She told me to stay away, but it's not a fight. She just doesn't want me there overnight while her little brother's here, that's all."

"Little brother?"

"Yeah. Dub. He's visiting from Arkansas."

Dub came as news to Gwen. She hadn't even known that Tess had a brother, but then she realized that she knew next to nothing about Tess's early years in the backwoods of the Ozarks. That was due largely to Ron Chrome.

"Tess's hillbilly years got no value," Chrome once told her. "They're excess baggage for the trip she's on. As far as the world's concerned, her life started when she got to Nashville."

Gwen wondered now if Chrome knew that some of Tess's excess baggage was in town. "So how old is Dub?" she asked.

Seth shrugged. "Eight or nine."

"And how long's he staying?"

Another shrug. "Tess thought about a week, but it's not like she's sure." A pause. "And it's not like she's too happy about it, either."

"How's that?"

"I don't know. She's just kinda bitchy."

Tess being bitchy wasn't news, and Gwen put the matter out of her thoughts until the next day at the office when she was discussing a coming promotion for Tess's new movie, and she happened to mention Dub's visit to Chrome.

"What?" Chrome had been leaning over his desk, studying a spread of photos, but now he came bolt upright. "How long's he been here?"

Gwen was surprised by Chrome's reaction, and she hesitated a moment. "I...I'm not sure. A few days, I think."

"Damn it! Why wasn't I told about this?"

"I just found out yesterday, Ron. And...and I didn't think it was all that important."

"How long's he staying?"

"Seth thought a week, but he wasn't sure."

"Son of a bitch!" Chrome pounded a fist on the desk and glowered down at the photos. After a moment, he looked up. "You'd better run out to Tess's house, Toddy. Find out for sure how long he's staying, and tell Tess that...what's his name again?"

"Dub."

"And tell Tess that Dub keeps a low profile. I don't want him showing up anyplace where he can get media attention. And remind her that's just about everywhere in this town. And make sure she knows these instructions are coming straight from me."

Gwen was confused. "I don't understand all the fuss, Ron. What's the big deal about a visit from her little brother?"

He stared for a long moment before answering. "Sometimes little things can turn into a big deal. If I've learned anything in this business, it's that. And we've invested a lot of time and effort in Tess's image of late. We've made a helluva lot of progress too, and I don't wanna screw that up by suddenly adding hillbilly to the mix."

"Well, she did start as a country singer, Ron. People don't expect her to come from the Hamptons."

"Look, Toddy, just chalk it up to micromanaging, okay? So I'm a control freak. Humor me. And get out to Tess's house, okay?"

Half an hour later, Gwen was standing at Tess's front door. She rang the bell three times before Tess opened the door with a glass in her hand. Tess's eyes were unfocused, and Gwen assumed that the glass held booze and that it wasn't Tess's first drink of the day. "What the hell you want?" Tess slurred. "We're not shooting today. This is 'sposed to be my day off."

"Ron asked me to come."

Tess rolled her eyes. "Yeah, what's Mother Chrome want now?"

"It's about your brother."

Tess's eyes focused suddenly. "What about him? And how'd you even find out that he's here?"

"Seth mentioned it."

"Son of a bitch!" Tess took a quick sip from her glass. "So what's Motherfucker Chrome want with my brother? He gonna take him to Disneyland?"

"He…he sent some instructions. May I come in, Tess?"

Tess hesitated and then stepped back, letting Gwen into the foyer. "So let's hear my instructions."

"He just wants you to keep a low profile while your brother's here. No media attention."

Tess snorted. "So what's my brother, the goddamn plague or something?"

"Ron just doesn't want any distractions from your current publicity campaign."

"Yeah, right." Tess took another sip. "Is that all?"

"Ron also wants to know how long Dub's staying."

"Till I'm ready for him to go, that's how long. Now if you don't mind, this *is* my day off."

Gwen turned for the door and then noticed movement over Tess's shoulder. She turned back as a slender, blonde-haired boy walked into the room. The family resemblance was strong. This surely was Dub, and his sullen expression tied him to Tess as well. "Hi, Dub. I'm Gwen Todd from your sister's agency. It's nice to meet you."

Dub stared without a word or a change of expression, and after a moment, he turned and left the room.

Tess watched him go and then turned to Gwen. "He's shy. Just like me." Tess cackled at this before adding, "And you can tell Mother Chrome that he's keeping a low profile, that he won't even talk to you."

CHAPTER 21

▼

L. R. Todd stood puzzling in the middle of his basement, trying to remember why he'd come down there. For that matter, he didn't even remember coming down, nor could he recall how long he'd been there. It was as if he'd been asleep, and now he was stumbling up through the foggy zone that separates slumber from wakefulness. He'd been too much in that fog of late, it was a troubling place, not restful like sleep. And he had thoughts, many thoughts, but they wouldn't connect, and they clanged away in his head like an orchestra where each instrument played a different tune.

L. R. closed his eyes and tried to sort his thoughts, hoping for a connection that might lead him though the fog. After several moments, a single thought separated from the jumble, a trumpet sounding over the dissonance: toilet. Yes, toilet. The toilet upstairs was plugged. Plunger. Yes, plunger. He'd come to the basement for a plunger. Ah, the joy of lucid thought.

Now, where was the plunger? He scanned his workbench. He looked beneath it. He turned and looked beneath the stairs where several crates were stacked. He moved one crate, then another, and then his dark, bushy eyebrows knitted in confusion. His mind had been clutching tightly to the plunger thought, and now it took a moment to let go and grasp a new thought: shotgun. He picked up the gun. It was a twelve-gauge pump, and he knew it was his, his hands remembering as much as his mind. He worked the pump and inspected the chamber, noting it was empty, and then he worked the pump again, closing the action. The familiar feel of the gun in his hands was good, and he worked the pump twice more, and suddenly new thoughts began connecting like soldiers running from a barracks to form ranks. He recalled steam rising from his coffee on cold mornings in a duck blind; he could almost hear the burr of beating wings as a cock pheasant flushed from golden corn on a brilliant autumn afternoon.

The peace of connected thought settled over L. R., but then a question broke through the ranks. Why was the shotgun under the stairs? It didn't belong there. It belonged in the cabinet where he kept his other hunting gear. He turned now and crossed to that cabinet and opened its doors. The gun case hung empty where the gun should have been. L. R. looked at the gun in his hands. He must have put it under the stairs in one of his foggier moments, and that troubled him. Guns shouldn't be left lying around. He then inspected the other gear in the cabinet, taking satisfaction from the fact that at least everything else seemed to be in its proper place. His camo hunting jacket hung from a peg and next to it his hunting cap. There were heavy woolen socks and lace-up boots. There was a set of duck calls. No ammo, though. Where was the ammo?

Then L. R. remembered. He always stored the ammo separate from the gun. It was the responsible thing to do. He turned to his workbench and nodded. Yes, the small cupboard above the bench was where he kept the ammo. It was satisfying to remember a responsible thing, and his satisfaction deepened when he opened the cupboard and found several boxes of shotgun shells. He took one of the boxes from the cupboard and inspected it. Number 1 shot. Too big a load for pheasants; too big for ducks, for that matter. He'd probably bought them for geese. He shrugged and took three shells from the box and slipped them into the magazine, then he pumped a shell into the chamber, remembering to set the safety. His hands had performed this sequence of action almost without thought, instinctive steps that gave pleasure, and L. R. suddenly knew that pleasure would be greater yet were he in a field or slough with his gun, rather than standing in his basement.

It was hot outside. Hot July weather didn't go with the shotgun as well as crisp fall weather would, but still it was better to be outside. He crossed the yard and entered the grove. The grove was shady and cooler, and he walked easily with the gun cradled in his left arm. The grove was also where L. R. stored mementos from the past: a rusting corn planter, the chassis of an old Dodge pickup, an old stove. These were things L. R. couldn't bring himself to throw away, things he might find a use for some-day, and the grove was the perfect place to store them, and now they gave him comfort.

At the other side of the grove, he stepped back into the sun and heat, but there was no thought of returning to the shade. He had reached his sweet corn patch. The one-acre patch was tucked in a corner, with the grove on two sides and his renter's soybean field on the other two sides. It was an ideal place for a sweet corn patch. For one thing, it was a hot spot. The grove trapped warm air, preventing summer breezes from blowing it away, and the warm air hastened the corn's ripening. For another thing, the patch was nearly a quarter mile from the county road, and more importantly, the grove hid it from view. L. R. still worried about pilfering, though. Goddamn city folks would go to great lengths to steal a man's property.

He stepped into the patch and paused to savor the straight rows. There were thirty-six rows in all, divided into twelve rows of three different vari-eties. The varieties were easily discerned by variations in tassel color and stalk height, and the variety closest to the grove, where L. R. now stood, was the earliest, the first to ripen. L. R. and his neighbors had been eating that variety for over a week, and now he inspected an ear and saw that the recent heat had pushed it beyond its prime. Another day or two of this heat, and it would start to dent. He moved further into the patch, into the middle twelve rows. Here he found what he called young roasting ears, good eating, but still a few days away from prime. And L. R. knew without looking that in the outermost planting he would find ears with translucent blisters for kernels, ears still ten days from the table. All this certainty of pedigree and all this orderliness of straight rows pleased L. R., as did the shotgun cradled in his arm. It all connected and comforted.

He moved three rows further into the middle planting, and there his pleasure and comfort ended abruptly. Broken stalks, stalks stripped of their ears, lay in a tangle on the ground, disorder in the midst of order. There were footprints in the soft soil too. Someone had been in his patch. Goddamn city folks! It had to be. L. R. knew that he hadn't picked any corn from the middle planting yet, and he was equally sure that none of his neighbors had, either. They wouldn't make such a mess. Nor would Gwen, and no one else had asked permission, so someone had been in there without permission. Goddamn city folks, thrashing around like bulls, breaking stalks, and defiling order.

He swung his gaze to his left, then to his right, and then he turned completely around. He sensed that he wasn't alone. He brought the gun to the ready position and turned slowly again. Then he stood perfectly still and listened. He listened hard and long, but the only sound was the slight rustle of corn leaves in the light breeze. It was hot standing there in the sun, and sweat beaded on his forehead and trickled down his back beneath his shirt, but still he watched and listened, his finger resting on the gun's safety button. Finally, after another long minute, L. R. turned and walked slowly to the grove, pausing twice to watch and listen. When he reached the grove, its coolness did nothing to ease his anger boiling inside. It was the same every year, just when the sweet corn reached its prime. He would have to remain vigilant in the days ahead. Goddamn city folks!

CHAPTER 22

▼

By ten o'clock that morning, Howard Cronk had liberated Hester's eight-foot crucifix from the plumbing supplies at the back of the garage, stripped away the plastic, and dusted Scottish Jesus. He didn't really need dusting—the plastic had done its job—but Hester had insisted, and if she'd had her way, it would've been done two hours earlier. That hadn't happened because Nellie Murphy had somehow washed her dentures down the garbage disposal, where they had become stuck, and Howard was then called to rescue them. He'd accomplished this by nine o'clock, and if he'd had his way, he would've then moved on to Lloyd Perkins' house, where he was to install a new shower. But of course, he didn't have his way. Hester conceded Nellie's dentures to be an emergency, but Lloyd's shower could wait. With few exceptions, the Lord's work trumped plumbing.

Now the crucifix stood on its wooden base at the center of the garage, and Howard looked Scottish Jesus in the eye. "Hester's zealous. I understand that, and most of the time I reckon it's a good thing. I don't expect her to change, but would it hurt much if once in a while she got horny instead?"

"Um, excuse me."

Howard whirled around to face the man now standing in the open garage doorway, and his surprise quickly turned to embarrassment at having been caught talking to a statue. "Who are you?"

The man was balding and fat, and his heavy jowls sagged around his bow tie. "H. Landon Beard, attorney at law." He held out a business card. "I'm here to see Senator Cronk."

Howard eyed the man for a moment and then studied the card. This would be the guy that called Hester the night before and got her all worked up over this cult business. Howard had been prepared to dislike the man, and now that he was here, Howard's dislike exceeded all expectations. To begin with, Howard distrusted lawyers, and this one had the look of a bottom-feeder. "Specializing in personal injury," the card read. That was a warning flag for Howard, as was the aging Cadillac with rusting fenders parked in the driveway. Then there was the bow tie. Howard despised bow ties and the men who wore them, and on top of all that, Beard had just caught him speaking of his sexual desires to Scottish Jesus.

"Is she expecting you?" Howard asked.

"Yes, I spoke with her on the phone last night and again just an hour ago." Beard's tone was patronizing, and it became more so when he asked, "Do you work for the senator?"

"I'm her husband," said Howard without trying to mask the edge in his voice.

"Good for you. Now if you'd be kind enough to tell her I'm here."

"Wait here." Howard was a well-mannered person and normally would have invited a caller into the house, but now he took a measure of delight in leaving Beard to cool his heels in the garage.

Howard found Hester in her study, talking on the phone, and when he held up Beard's card, she waved him off and continued talking.

"Yes…Yes…Yes, I understand what you're saying, Tom, but I must tell you that I completely disagree. The Founding Fathers never intended the First Amendment to protect satanic cults…No, Tom, I'm not putting words in your mouth…Tom…Tom, if you'd just let me speak to the governor. I think I'm entitled to that…We're all busy, Tom. It's an election year, after all, but if anyone should understand the importance of this issue to our base, it ought to be the governor…Tom…Tom, this is getting us nowhere. Just tell the governor two things. One, he can't hide behind the

First Amendment on this one, and two, I expect a call from him person-ally. Good-bye."

Hester hung up the phone and shook her head. "Petty tyrant. Who does he think he is? Just because he's chief of staff doesn't entitle him to run the whole state. He wasn't elected to anything." She looked up at Howard. "What is it?"

Howard held out H. Landon Beard's card. "This guy's here to see you."

Hester looked at the card. "Oh, Mr. Beard. Why didn't you say so? Show him in."

Howard turned to leave.

"Wait, Howard. I think the living room'll be better. Show him there. And I want you to sit in too."

Howard had been afraid of that. "I was gonna head over to Lloyd Per-kins' place and work on his shower."

"No, that can wait. I want you involved in this. We'll probably need logistical support."

Howard sighed. Logistical support usually involved his pickup and the transportation of Scottish Jesus. Suddenly, his plumbing prospects for the days ahead looked bleak.

He went back to the garage and led Beard in through the kitchen to the living room, where Hester stood waiting to greet them. She looked quite senatorial, and at the same time quite lovely, in a smart green pantsuit. In contrast, Beard looked every bit the sleazy lawyer in his ill-fitted suit and silly bow tie. Howard was something of a contrast himself. He wore jeans and a khaki shirt with "Cronk Plumbing & Heating" stitched over the pocket, not the usual attire for a high-powered political powwow, but then he had no interest in powwows, political or otherwise. Hester extended a gracious hand, welcoming Beard, then she asked him to be seated, and to Howard's further consternation, the lawyer sat in Howard's recliner. Hes-ter sat on the sofa, and Howard settled in the old rocker that always creaked as if it were about to break whenever he sat in it.

"Let me begin by thanking you for bringing this to my attention, Mr. Beard," said Hester. "Something like this happening in my district is never welcome news, but still it's important that I know about it."

"I'd have called you even if it were another district, Senator. When it comes to ugly stuff like this, you're the people's choice. You're the one who looks out for the regular folks."

Hester nodded, acknowledging the compliment, and opened her notebook. "Please tell me again, Mr. Beard, how you learned of all this. And I need specifics."

H. Landon Beard leaned forward and spoke in a confidential tone. "Well, I first went out to the Cox place three days ago to look into this Sphinx business—"

"What brought you out there?" Hester interrupted. "Did Gabby Cox call you?"

Beard seemed surprised by the question. "Why, yes, of course. I wouldn't have gone out there if he hadn't called."

"And why did Mr. Cox call you?"

"Well, he thought he might need a lawyer. This Sphinx thing's pretty complicated, you know, what with insurance companies and a federal investigation and all."

"And did Mr. Cox hire you?"

"Well, I thought it best to look into the matter a bit before committing myself. I'm rather particular about the cases I take on. I told Mr. Cox that I'd check a few things out and get back to him."

"And did you?"

"Yes, the very next day, and to my great shock, the commune had moved in and—"

"Just one moment, Mr. Beard." Hester held up a hand. "What you described to me on the phone last night was a cult, not a commune."

Beard shrugged. "Cult, commune, what's the difference?"

"There's a great deal of difference, Mr. Beard, and we won't succeed against these people if we allow them to hide behind soft labels. That's what liberals do: obfuscate with fuzzy language. 'Commune' doesn't begin to convey the evil here. Let's be clear from the start: we're talking about a cult."

Beard nodded so enthusiastically that his jowls bounced. "I take your point, Senator. You're absolutely right. This is a hippie cult alright, and—"

"No, no, no, Mr. Beard. Surely they aren't hippies. Hippies are so passé. What you described to me are Satanists."

"I did?"

Hester eyed Beard for a moment. "I've dedicated my whole life to fighting evil. I know a satanic cult when I see one."

"Well, yes, of course, Senator. You're the one with the expertise here. I'll certainly defer to your judgment."

Hester acknowledged this with another nod. "Now then, Mr. Beard, just how many Satanists are out there?"

"When I left two days ago, there were four of 'em, not counting Cox."

"Four?"

Howard, watching from the rocker, sensed Hester's disappointment, and he wasn't surprised. He knew his wife would take on Satanists however she found them, one at a time if necessary, but this was an election year, and in an election year, the more Satanists the merrier.

"In our phone conversation last night you led me to understand that the number was larger," said Hester, "certainly more than four."

"When I left two days ago, there were four," said Beard, "but I believe their numbers have grown significantly."

"But you haven't been back since?"

"No, Senator, when I saw those hip…when I saw those Satanists, I decided right then and there that I wasn't going to have anything to do with them. That's not my style of lawyering."

"Yet you believe their numbers are growing?"

"Yes. I decided against representing Cox, but that doesn't mean I won't involve myself from higher ground. I feel a moral duty here, Senator. That's why I called you. And I've also had conversations with others in town, and it's those conversations that lead me to believe there're a lot more'n four out there now."

"Who else have you talked to?"

"Well, for one there's Slade Walters. He was out there two nights ago, just hours after me, and their numbers had grown by a bunch already. He was jumped by at least ten of 'em."

"Slade Walters?" Hester raised an eyebrow.

"Yes, ma'am. He's a local pilot."

"I know who Slade Walters is, Mr. Beard. He's rather coarse, as a matter of fact." Hester thought a moment and then shrugged. "But then, God works in mysterious ways, and Slade Walters wouldn't be the first coarse person he's chosen to do his work."

Jesus, thought Howard. The idea of Slade Walters being among God's chosen wasn't comforting.

Hester continued. "And who else have you talked to?"

"Just some of Slade's, ah, friends down at the Legion Club," said Beard.

"Do you believe that Slade and the others would be willing to join in a struggle against this evil?"

Beard nodded. "Yes, Senator, I get the feeling that folks are real upset about this. They want to do something, but they need leadership and direction, and that's why I called you."

Hester smiled and pondered a moment. "I see a two-pronged effort, Mr. Beard. First, we need statewide attention focused here, from government officials and the media too. I've already begun working on that. My office in St. Paul will issue a press release this afternoon, and I spoke with the governor just before you arrived."

Humph, thought Howard.

"You were right to call me, Mr. Beard. If anyone can bring statewide pressure to bear, it's me, but we also need local, grassroots involvement. That's the second prong, and it's vital to our success. Can you see yourself involved in that effort, Mr. Beard?"

"Yes, Senator, I stand ready to help in any way I can."

Hester nodded. "And how do you think that might be? What role do you see for yourself?"

Yeah, thought Howard, *that's what I want to know. What's in it for you, Beard?*

Beard thought a moment. "Mostly, I'm motivated by a sense of moral duty here, but if there's an expertise that I bring to the party, I suppose it's my legal background. I can certainly help out with any questions of law."

"And would you expect to be paid for those services?" asked Hester.

Beard hesitated. "Well, I certainly don't intend to profit from this…but of course, there'll be expenses and…"

"Of course, Mr. Beard. I don't expect you to lose money." Hester thought a moment. "Actually, our cause and my reelection campaign are about the same thing. It's the same struggle. This cult is properly a focal point for the campaign, so I don't see why we can't consider you to be a campaign worker and reimburse you from my campaign funds."

Beard pondered only a second. "That's sound thinking, Senator, and I'd be greatly honored to be a part of your organization. I've long admired your leadership. You're the people's choice."

Hester considered this and then smiled. "Actually, Mr. Beard, I'm God's choice."

Howard sighed. He and Scottish Jesus would soon be hitting the road.

CHAPTER 23

▼

"Corn sucks," said Tanner Mills, "and that's all you got out here, mile after boring mile of corn."

Gwen Todd was sitting in the passenger seat of Tanner's car, and she gave him a weary look. Tanner could be funny and charming, as he had been the night before, as he had been fifteen minutes earlier when he picked her up at the library, but in a flash he could turn into a grouch, as he was now, complaining about corn of all things.

"We have soybeans too," she said, pointing ahead to an upcoming field, "and wheat."

"If you think soybeans are an exciting change of pace, then you're seriously in need of a life. God, it sucks!"

"Well, Tanner, if life's so dull out here, I guess there's no point in going out to dinner tonight. You'll only get bored."

"But now that I think of it, corn does have a certain...what?...bohemian quality about it. Look at that field over there. It reminds me of, um, Paris. Yeah, definitely Paris, and what delightful beans."

Gwen shook her head. She was having second thoughts about accompanying Tanner out to Gabby Cox's farm. She hoped it wouldn't go badly, and she wasn't sure which offered the greater risk, a charming Tanner or a grouchy one. It probably didn't matter. She'd called Gabby that morning to let him know that she was bringing Tanner out, and he had received the news with little enthusiasm, leaving her with the impression that if anyone else had asked, the answer would've been no.

"Take the next right," she said, directing him off the highway onto the county road.

Tanner slowed and turned onto the gravel. "So you met these people in the commune the other night, right?"

"Yes, and it's not a commune. Remember what you said about getting the truth out. Don't start by chasing goofy rumors just to make your story interesting."

"If it's not a commune, then what is it?"

Gwen chuckled. "They're Shriners."

"Shriners? You mean the guys in the red hats?"

She chuckled again. "No, they're just Sphinx fans. Young and harmless Sphinx fans."

"Then why'd you call 'em Shriners?"

"Because…never mind. It's not important. It's just something Gabriel came up with that's kind of cute, but the main thing is, it's not a commune or anything like that. They're just kids who idolized a rock star. Not the smartest thing, maybe, but then, they aren't the first to do it, and they won't be the last."

Tanner shrugged. "Idolizing a rock star's not that stupid."

Gwen looked at him, surprised. "So who'd you idolize at that age?"

"Me? No one. Except Mencken, of course."

"Yeah, right."

"But I know stupid when I see it. I cover the capitol, after all, and a kid idolizing a rock star is way down on the list compared to some of the stuff those jokers pull."

"Here we are," said Gwen. "This is the Cox place."

Tanner slowed and turned down the driveway, and as the yard came into view, so did the charred ruins of the barn. Tanner whistled. "So this is where old Sphinx and Sparkle bought it. It's a long way from the limelight."

"Actually, the limelight's pretty portable, Tanner, as you should know from all the coverage this mess has gotten. And while we're on the subject,

Gabby's shy—he doesn't like the limelight—so behave yourself, Mr. Reporter."

"Me? I'm just a simple seeker of truth."

*   *   *   *

"So, have you known Gwen long?" Tanner asked. He and Gabby were standing next to the burnt barn, and the question was small talk aimed at getting past Gabby's hostility. That hostility had been apparent from the start. Tanner had parked in the yard, and as Gwen had climbed from the car, Gabby had come out from the house. His face had lit up when he saw her face, and then it had gone dark a moment later when Tanner got out. Now Tanner wondered if Gwen Todd was the wrong small talk, the wrong button to push with this man. Thus far, their conversation had been marked by one-word responses and long silences, and after another such silence, Gabby finally answered.

"Reckon I've known her most all my life. We were neighbors. She grew up just a mile over." Gabby nodded to the west and then fixed his gaze on Tanner. "What's that got to do with this Sphinx business?"

Tanner shrugged. "Just background. If I'm gonna write about you, I need to know more than just your name, rank, and serial number."

"Maybe I don't want you writing about me. Maybe there's been way too much written already. This story's done, so maybe it's time you folks just left me alone."

The hostility wasn't going away. It was there in Gabby's eyes and his words and his tone of voice, and Tanner now wondered if it was a good idea to talk with Gabby alone. He was a different person with Gwen around. She softened him. Tanner looked across the yard to where Gwen sat on the porch, talking with Teal Osborne and Meredith Towne. He might yet need her help in getting Gabby to open up, he thought.

"Look, Mr. Cox, I sympathize with you. The media can be a pain in the ass, and I don't claim to be an exception. It's no fun, but truth be known, this story's not done, much as you'd like it to be. Sphinx and Sparkle crashing into your barn was just the start, and all that's happened since is a continuation of the story."

A look of horror came across Gabby's face. "But it's gotta end somewhere. It can't go on like this forever."

"Yeah, you're right. It'll die down eventually, but when you have a pop culture icon like Sphinx involved and you have lots of national media attention, it'll die pretty hard. And even after it does die down, there'll be a different aura attached to this place. People'll remember, and they'll wanna come here, and they'll figure they've got a right to do that—people like the mob that trampled your corn. They acted like they owned the place, didn't they?"

"And they were wrong," Gabby bristled. "I own it, and it's time folks started respecting that."

Tanner nodded toward the camper. "What about them? What about the Shriners? They're a part of the story too, and they seem to be here with your blessing."

"That don't make it anybody else's business. Who I choose to let camp on my land is my business."

"Well, you may be right again, but that won't stop people from making it their business. There're people in town who are doing just that, and some are saying that you've started a commune out here."

Gabby's eyes flashed with anger. "Goddamn that Slade Walters! He's behind that kinda talk, and it's all wrong. This ain't no commune. You can see that for yourself. It's just four young people who came to see where their idol died."

"And that's all there are? Just four?"

Gabby nodded. "The two girls there with Gwen. Jack and Kevin, the two guys, took my pickup to town for supplies."

"By some accounts in town, there're dozens of 'em out here, and those same accounts include talk of drugs and weird religious rituals."

Gabby's mouth opened, but no words came out; he shook his head instead.

"It's a helpless feeling," said Tanner, "I understand that. It's hard to get the truth out with a lot of rumors flying around. Given a choice, people usually go for the sensational over the truth, but maybe I can help with that."

"How?"

"By getting the story right. By getting the truth out."

Gabby looked skeptical. "If no one else can stop the rumors, what makes you think you can?"

"The *Star Tribune*'s a respected newspaper with a wide readership, and if I must say so myself, I'm a pretty good reporter. I'll get it right. I think it's your best chance."

Gabby thought a moment. "How long've you known Gwen?"

Tanner hesitated before answering, realizing once more that association with Gwen Todd was his only hope of gaining Gabby's trust. He decided that the truth was the best course. "I just met her yesterday. I stopped at the library looking for information, and she agreed to help. Mostly because you're a friend." He didn't mention that he'd had dinner with Gwen the night before or that he hoped to again that night, sensing that extent of the truth might not be helpful.

"And Gwen's okay with this? She thinks I oughta talk to you?"

Tanner nodded toward the house. "We can go ask her if you like."

Gabby thought another moment. "Okay, what do you wanna know?"

*   *   *   *

Gwen sat in one of the rockers on Gabby's porch, half listening to Teal Osborne chatter about Sphinx and half watching Tanner and Gabby, standing across the yard. She worried again that it'd been a mistake to bring Tanner out here, and she tried to read their body language to get a sense of how things were going. Mostly their body language spoke of tension, and then her thoughts were pulled back to the porch as Teal broke into song.

Baby, baby, come ride my cloud,
We'll slip the Earth and fly so proud,
We'll soar so high, we'll have it all,

Higher and higher and higher,
So high that we can never fall.

Teal's voice faltered on the final line, and she fell silent as tears welled in her eyes. Meredith Towne reached over and patted her knee. "Easy, Teal."

Teal sobbed. "I can't help it. 'Cloud Rider' is just so...so holy!"

"Easy," Meredith said again. "It's just a song."

Teal looked at Meredith with horror. "Just a song! How can you say that, Meredith? It's so much more than a song. It's...it's a gospel. It's a beacon for the spirit."

Meredith glanced at Gwen before saying, "Let's keep things in perspective, okay, Teal?"

Teal's eyes flashed with anger now. "Perspective! You're the one who's, like, lost perspective. You're the one losing touch with your spirit. Maybe you've forgotten why we came here in the first place. Maybe you've, like, sold out and bought into your daddy's capitalist religion."

That hung in the air for an uneasy moment before Meredith said, "Don't go there, Teal."

Teal dabbed her eyes. "I'm...I'm sorry, Mere. It's just that my emotions are so raw. My spirit's, like, exhausted." She paused and then stood. "I think I need to be alone for a while."

Meredith and Gwen watched Teal cross the yard, and when she disappeared into the camper, Meredith said, "Sorry about that. Teal gets a little carried away."

Gwen shrugged and smiled. "Nothing wrong with a little youthful exuberance. Not Teal's kind anyway. I don't see that it hurts anything."

"Perhaps not," said Meredith, "but when she gets off on her Sphinx-Jesus thing, it doesn't help much, either. It's a waste of time."

"I gathered the other night when you said—what was your expression, 'Teal's little metaphysical leaps?'—that you don't see Sphinx as the second coming."

Meredith laughed. "Of course not. His music's great, and it is spiritual in a way, and driving out here's been a kick, but give me credit for some depth. Teal's a sweetie and a friend, but she's not the deepest thinker around."

Gwen remembered that Meredith was the daughter of a Methodist minister. "So how *do* you feel about your father's…'capitalist religion'?"

"That's a waste of time too. Let's just say that my father and I haven't been communicating very well of late."

"So do you go with something else? Something other than the mainline churches?"

"I'm not into churches, period. Churches are all about religion, and religion's the cause of most of the world's trouble. They're supposed to help people connect with their spiritual side, but they're more likely to keep it from happening."

Gwen smiled. She found herself liking this round and serious girl more and more. "So for you, being spiritual is different from being religious?"

"Well, yeah, of course." Meredith's manner and tone suggested that the point should have been obvious. "Religion's just so…so man-made. It can't work without a bunch of bylaws and rules, and it's always run by grouchy old men, and if you don't follow the bylaws and rules, you go to Hell." She laughed. "You know what religion is like? A chain letter. Yeah, it's just like a chain letter. For a chain letter to work, it has to be passed on and on—that's what it's about—but pretty soon, the math gets impossible. Religion's like that. It sounds good at first, but a religion has to evangelize to stay in business, and pretty soon, both math and physics get in the way."

"And spirituality's different?"

"Yeah. To begin with, it's not man-made. It doesn't have the bylaws and rules. It's an internal thing, an individual thing; you don't have to evangelize, and if you don't smother it with religion, it can connect you with the world. It's really about harmony, about coming into harmony with the forces that flow through the universe, and you can only do that through your spiritual side. Religion won't work. Too many bylaws."

Gwen was increasingly intrigued by their conversation, though she suspected it was more a matter of intellectual stimulation than spiritual enlightenment. "So what are these forces flowing through the universe?"

Meredith pondered a moment. "They're the essence of life. I suppose some would call them God, but it'd be a mistake to assume they're all good. You only understand a force by how it's manifested, and that goes back to the idea that good versus evil is at the bottom of everything. In that sense, hate's a force, or the manifestation of some essential force, but then so is love, and if I agree with my father about anything, it's that God is love." She paused and then laughed. "Unless you're talking Hollywood-style love. Then you've got bylaws again."

Gwen nodded at this, recalling the bylaws of Hollywood love.

*   *   *   *

"Gabby doesn't talk much."

Gwen smiled at Tanner's observation. They were in his car again, driving back to town. "Don't take it personally. Gabriel Cox is a man of few words."

"That's the understatement of the day."

"But he did talk to you, right? You were standing over there by the barn for a long time."

Tanner shrugged. "Yeah, he talked."

"And was it helpful?"

Another shrug. "I suppose, but this story ain't gonna win no Pulitzer."

"Did you expect one?"

"A guy can hope."

"So what did you learn?"

Tanner thought a moment. "Two things for sure. One, he loved his barn. The guy actually misses the thing."

"Of course he does. I understand that. This is a three-generation family farm. The roots go pretty deep. What was the other thing you learned?"

"He's in love with you."

"Be serious, Tanner."

"I am serious. He's got the hots for you. Probably more so than for his barn."

"Well, thank you for that. It's always nice to be ranked ahead of a barn, but I think you're mistaken. Gabriel and I are just friends. He's a sweet, shy guy who used to be my neighbor, and now we chat when he comes to the library. That's about the extent of it."

"You were out at his place the other night, partying with him and the Shriners."

"That…just happened. It's not likely to happen again, and surely you can think of something to write about besides that."

"You're in denial about Cox. The way he feels about you is all over his face, but yeah, you're right, love's not the story here."

"What is the story?"

He stared down the road for a long moment before answering. "It's a witch's brew, Gwen. You've got intolerance and stupidity. There's hate and there's zealotry, all of humanity's finer traits. It's like Sphinx created a vacuum when he crashed into that barn, and it's an ugly vacuum that just sucks in ugly stuff."

Gwen thought about Meredith and her essential forces. "That sounds awful. Can't you find a more positive spin?"

Tanner glanced at her. "Spin? I thought I was supposed to get the story right, not spin a happy ending. And unfortunately I know ugly when I see it. I cover the capitol, remember?"

CHAPTER 24

▼

Kevin Calm glanced over Jack Sand's shoulder and said, "Maybe a beer wasn't such a hot idea."

They had borrowed Gabby's pickup to drive to town for supplies—junk food, beer, and condoms—and because the day was hot, they'd stopped for a cold one before going back to the farm. The afternoon crowd in the Legion Club was light, and Jack and Kevin sat in a booth, sipping from mugs of beer.

"Why not?" asked Jack without turning to look.

"Isn't that your favorite flying butthead over there?"

Jack turned now to scan the dimly lit room, and he recognized Slade Walters sitting at the far end of the bar. "And so it is, Hayesboro's answer to Charles Lindbergh, fueling up for his next flight, no doubt."

Kevin took a quick gulp of beer. "Let's get outta here, Jack."

"Why?"

"Because that asshole's trouble."

"Relax. Drink your beer. That sky cowboy ain't gonna do anything in here." Jack chuckled. "And maybe I oughta go over and see how he is. Last time I saw him, he wasn't doing all that good, but then I'd just knocked him on his ass."

"You hit him once, Jack. It was Gabby that took the starch out of him." Kevin glanced nervously in Slade's direction again. "Besides, he's on his home turf, and we're the strangers. It wouldn't be too smart to go looking for a fight in here."

"I'm not looking for a fight. And that fat boy's most likely had enough of me, so stop worrying, okay? I'll get you back to Meredith all safe and sound."

Kevin glared down at his beer. He hated it when Jack mocked his manliness, as he was clearly doing now, but as much as he hated Jack's mocking, he hated his own scrawny body too, and he also hated situations like this where his lack of physical presence seemed to hang out there for all to mock. "Let's just get outta here, okay?"

"When I finish my beer. Now relax, for chrissakes." Jack took a long sip and then turned confidently toward Slade again. "Say, now that's interesting."

"What?"

"The fat ass sitting next to the sky cowboy at the bar—isn't that the lawyer that tried to run us off that first day out at Gabby's?"

Kevin took a quick glance. "Looks like him. So what's so interesting about that?"

"Well, Gabby ran the lawyer off, and then that night he ran the sky cowboy off too, and now they're sitting there having this very serious discussion. Maybe they're planning something, like a little revenge out at Gabby's."

"Aw, jeez, Jack, your imagination's working overtime."

"So maybe you think those two are planning what they're gonna teach in Sunday school? I don't think so. Maybe we oughta get a little closer and get a listen to what they're talking about."

"And maybe it's time to stop with all the games and head back to New York."

"Just when things are getting interesting? Hell, Kev, those two could belong to the Klan. They could be planning to burn Gabby out."

Kevin rolled his eyes. "I don't think the Klan's real big in Minnesota, Jack."

"Well, there's that northern version—those guys that hang out in the sticks and shoot bankers and feds. The Posse something or other."

Kevin shook his head. "You've been watching too much TV." He raised his mug but stopped halfway to his mouth. "Uh oh."

"What?"

"They spotted us. The lawyer's pointing at us."

"So? We've got a right to be here. Just be cool."

"Yeah, well, you can tell that to the sky cowboy. Here he comes."

Jack leaned back in the booth and smiled confidently. "Fine, we'll just see what that fat boy's got to say."

As it turned out, Slade had little to say. When he was ten feet away, he grabbed a wooden chair from an empty table and then swung it in a high arc just as Jack turned. The chair crashed down with a sickening thud into the side of Jack's face.

*   *   *   *

"So what time should I pick you up for dinner?" asked Tanner. They were just coming into town, and he turned toward the library.

"Who said we were having dinner together?"

"C'mon, Gwen, don't make me face the dreaded Hayesboro night alone."

Gwen smiled. "Afraid of the dark, are we?"

"Afraid of the God-awful boredom. Now what time?"

Gwen wasn't about to say as much, but she'd enjoyed Tanner's company the night before, and she was looking forward to seeing him again that night. She was about to agree on a time when they turned another corner and came on the flashing lights of a Hayesboro police car parked outside the Legion Club.

"What's this?" said Tanner. "A crime wave in Hayesboro? Maybe someone stole a six-pack."

Gwen rolled her eyes, and then she saw Jack sitting on the curb in front of the club, holding a white towel to the side of his face. "Stop, Tanner. That's Jack."

Tanner braked. "Jack who?"

"Jack from the Shriners. Pull over."

Tanner pulled to the curb, and Gwen got out of the car and walked toward where a police officer was now talking to Jack. Tanner followed, but as they neared, the cop held up his hand. "Please step back, Ms. Todd. I'm questioning this here suspect."

"Suspect?" Gwen looked at Jack, and he returned her gaze and shrugged. She could see now that the white towel held ice, and she could also see that his right eye was swollen shut. "He looks more like a victim than a suspect."

"Ma'am, please," said the cop.

Tanner stepped forward, flashing his press credential. "Tanner Mills. *Star Tribune*. What's the deal here?"

As the cop turned from the town librarian to a member of the press, his manner hardened noticeably. "Step back! This is police business."

Gwen and Tanner retreated up the sidewalk a few yards, and suddenly, a very shaken Kevin Calm appeared at their side. "We weren't doing anything, Gwen. He hit Jack with a chair for no reason at all."

"Who hit Jack, Kevin?"

"That fat jerk that was out at Gabby's the other night."

"And who are you?" asked Tanner, pointing at Kevin.

"This is Kevin," said Gwen. "He's a Shriner too." She put her hand on Kevin's shoulder. "Tell me how it happened."

Kevin gave a helpless shrug. "We were just having a beer and minding our own business. We didn't say a single word, and that asshole just walked up and hit Jack with a chair."

Gwen looked around. "Where's Slade now?"

Kevin nodded toward the Legion Club. "Inside. Another cop's talking to him in there."

Tanner looked at Gwen. "Is this Slade person your gentleman friend we met at Ted's last night?"

"Yes," she said, then turned back to Kevin. "Don't worry, Kevin, the police'll sort this out. They've dealt with Slade before."

"But that lawyer's telling 'em that Jack started it, that he swung first."

"What lawyer?"

Kevin shrugged. "I don't know his name. He was out at Gabby's the day we got here and Gabby ran him off."

Gwen nodded and Tanner asked, "Local guy?"

Gwen shook her head. "No, if it's who I think it is he's some ambulance chaser from the cities. Where's the lawyer now, Kevin?"

"He's inside too."

Just then the door of the Legion Club opened and Sam Stack, the county sheriff, walked out.

"Sam!" called Gwen.

Sam turned their way with an irritated look that disappeared when he recognized Gwen. "Afternoon, Gwen."

"What's happening, Sam? What's going on in there?"

Sam shrugged. "Nothing's going on in there. It was just another bar fight and it's all over now."

"That's not what he says," said Tanner, pointing at Kevin.

"And who're you?" Sam asked.

"Tanner Mills. *Star Tribune*."

Sam looked less than pleased to have the press there, and being a good six inches taller than Tanner he took advantage of each inch to glare down at the shorter man for an intimidating moment. "I reckon the Hayesboro police'll sort it out."

"C'mon, Sam," Gwen broke in, "we're talking about Slade Walters here. You know what a goon he is. You can't possibly believe that he didn't start this. And I know Jack and Kevin. They're staying out at Gabriel Cox's and they're not troublemakers."

Sam snorted. "I know where they're staying, Gwen, and I'm also hearing some pretty strange stuff about what's going on out there."

"Those are baseless rumors, Sam. You've been around long enough to not fall for unsubstantiated junk like that."

Sam sighed. "Look, Gwen, we're inside the city limits. The Hayesboro police'll take care of this. It's their jurisdiction. Only reason I'm here is because I was in my car a block away when the call came in, so I responded, but now it's the city's problem."

"Will there be charges?" This from Tanner.

Sam shrugged. "I doubt it. Each one's accusing the other of starting it, and each one has a witness." He nodded toward Kevin. "The bartender didn't see it start, and it was a light afternoon crowd, and it *was* just a bar fight. If the city attorney prosecuted every bar fight, he wouldn't get anything else done, and the judge'd most likely dismiss it with a slap on the wrists anyway. Big waste of time all around."

"Yeah," said Tanner, "that's justice out here in the sticks: A big waste of time."

Sam glared at Tanner for a long moment and seemed about to speak, but instead, he turned and walked up the street to his car.

*   *   *   *

Tanner parked in front of the library and turned to Gwen. "So what time?"

Gwen stared ahead for a moment. "I'm not sure I feel like going out anymore."

"C'mon, Gwen. The sheriff's right. It was just a bar fight. Don't let it wreck your day."

She stared a moment longer. "Alright. Six o'clock. My house."

He smiled and nodded. "See you then. And I promise to be cheerful, and I won't make nasty comments about your fair city."

As Gwen reached for the door handle, Karen Burton, an assistant librarian, was walking briskly down the steps from the library, and when she recognized Gwen, she came over and spoke breathlessly through the open car window. "Gwen, did you hear about the big fight at the Legion Club?"

Gossip was Karen's chief pastime, but even so, Gwen was surprised that the news had traveled so fast. "Yes, I heard, and it was just a bar fight," she said, using Sam Stack's words.

"Just a bar fight? I don't think so. Your basic Hayesboro bar brawl doesn't usually involve a satanic cult."

"Where did you hear that?"

"It's all over town. I'm surprised you haven't heard about it. People have been talking about all this strange stuff going on out at Gabby Cox's place, and now there's this fight. We might make the TV news out of the cities."

Karen hurried off, brimming with cult excitement, and Tanner glanced at Gwen. "Word travels fast around here."

"It's a small town."

"I suppose." Tanner thought a moment. "Still, I can feel the witch's brew in this. It's like someone's managing the message."

Gwen shuddered. She knew about managed messages.

CHAPTER 25

▼

Gwen Todd woke in the middle of the night to someone pounding on her apartment door. Her sleep had been deep, and it took nearly a minute for her to work her way up through the fog to the realization that the pounding was not a dream. She went to the door and warily called out, asking who was there. It was Seth Rawlings. His voice was strained, and he pleaded for her to let him in. Gwen opened the door, and he rushed into the room, his eyes wild, his face contorted with anguish.

"Seth, do you know what time it is?"

He ignored her question and stammered, "It's...it's awful, Gwen. You gotta help me. I...I didn't know where else to go."

Gwen had the sudden uneasy feeling that whatever had happened somehow involved Tess Snow, but at the moment, Seth seemed too distraught to be coherent. He needed to calm down. She also realized that she was wearing only panties and a T-shirt. He had seen her in much less, of course, but those days were over. "Sit down, Seth. Take some deep breaths while I get a robe. Do you want some water?"

He nodded and sank onto the sofa.

Gwen went to her bedroom and put on a robe and then walked to the kitchen, where she drank a half glass of water before refilling it for Seth. Back in the living room, she found him with his face buried in his hands, and when she touched his shoulder, he jumped as if she'd touched him with an electric wire. He drank half the water in two gulps and then paused to sigh deeply before finishing the water. His face was calmer now, but his eyes still darted anxiously from side to side.

"Take another minute," she said. "Try to relax, then tell me what happened."

He nodded meekly and leaned back against the sofa, his face tilted upward, his eyes closed. Gwen sat in the stuffed chair opposite him and watched the rise and fall of his chest gradually slow as his breathing became more regular. She had never seen him so upset, but now he seemed to be calming down. Her gaze shifted to take in her surroundings. Her apartment was a quiet, calming place, a refuge in the night. The living room was dimly lit by a single lamp, and soft sea air from the beach a block away wafted warmly through an open window as the faint tinkle of halyards from Marina del Rey provided gentle night music.

Her gaze returned to Seth, but she waited another minute before saying in a soft voice, "Tell me what happened."

He opened his eyes. They were calmer now, his great anxiety replaced by what seemed to Gwen a great sadness. He took a deep breath. "Tess…Tess's brother showed up today."

"Her brother?" Gwen was confused. "But Dub got here last week."

"No, another brother. Her older brother. Gilly."

"How many brothers does she have?"

Seth shrugged.

"So where's this Gilly from?"

"Arkansas. Same as…same as Dub."

Gwen was still confused. "What were you doing there, anyway? I thought Tess told you to stay away while Dub's here."

"She changed her mind. Dub got to know me at the beach, and we got along, so Tess had me come by the house the last couple days. Dub and me'd swim in the pool and stuff, and that way, Tess didn't have to entertain him. You know how Tess can be."

"Yeah, Seth, I know how Tess can be. So this…this Gilly just showed up today? Was Tess expecting him?"

"No way. He just drove up in his pickup. Said he'd come to take Dub home, and he and Tess started in fighting right away."

"Why? I thought Tess wasn't all that happy having Dub around. I would've thought she'd be happy to see him go."

Seth shrugged. "I got the feeling that Tess and Gilly would fight about whether the sun's gonna come up. I think they hate each other. They fought something awful."

"And they started in as soon as he got there?"

Seth nodded. "Tess'd been drinking, so she already had some attitude going, and you know how she can get. Hell, she's mean enough cold sober, but put some booze or dope in her, and look out. Then Gilly showed up, and he started in on the whiskey right away, and I'll tell you, Gwen, that son of a bitch is every bit as mean as Tess."

That Tess was a mean drunk didn't come as news to Gwen, nor was she surprised that Tess's older brother was just as mean, but something here felt completely wrong, and Gwen then realized that it was Seth's reaction. Seth was also perfectly aware of Tess's temperament. He had witnessed enough of her tantrums, so why was he now so distraught? There must be more, Gwen thought. Something else must have happened.

"Is there something you're not telling me?" she asked.

He looked at her now, and she saw fear in his eyes again. "I…I can't tell you, Gwen. I wanna tell you. That's why I came here, but I just can't."

"Why not, Seth? Why can't you tell me?"

He cast his eyes downward. "Because I'm afraid that if I tell you, if I tell anyone, it'll make it true. I want it to be a bad dream. I wanna wake up and know it never happened, but if I tell you, that'll make it real."

"What happened, Seth?"

He kept his gaze downward and spoke in little more than a whisper. "Dub's dead."

For a long moment, the only sound was the faint tinkle of halyards from the marina, now sadder music. "How?" she asked. "Was it an accident?" Her question was hopeful, but she feared the answer.

Seth shook his head. "He got shot. Dub got shot."

"Oh, dear God, Seth! Who shot him?"

"I…I'm not sure."

"You're not sure? Listen, Seth, take a deep breath—take several. Then tell me what happened. Try to remember everything."

Seth did as he was told, and after several deep breaths, he looked at Gwen. "I was out by the pool. Dub and I were watching TV and trying to ignore Tess and Gilly, but that was pretty hard to do. They were inside the house, but they were yelling so loud that we could hear everything. They'd been going on like that for hours and...and...God, Gwen, the things they said were so hurtful, so awful."

"Well, what were they fighting about?"

He paused and looked away before answering. "Dub."

"They were fighting about Dub?"

Seth nodded. "And he could hear it all, all the awful things they said, and finally he couldn't take it anymore, and he got up and started into the house. I told him not to go. I told him he should stay out of it, but he just looked at me. He had this scary look on his face like he was really pissed and really sad at the same time. Then he went into the house."

"What happened then, Seth?"

"Then I could hear all three of 'em fighting, and I just decided that I'd had enough, that I was gonna leave, but before I could, there...there was a shot."

Gwen pressed her knuckles to her mouth. "What did you do then?"

He shrugged. "Nothing. I just sat there. I froze, I guess. I didn't know what to do, and then Gilly came running outta the house. When he saw me, he stopped, but he didn't say anything. He took off running again and ran around the house, and then I heard his pickup start up, and he drove off."

"Then what?"

"Then I finally went in and...and there was Dub, in the middle of the living room floor, shot in the head. There was blood everywhere. It was awful, Gwen."

"Where was Tess?"

"That was awful too. She was just sitting in a chair not ten feet from Dub. She was just sitting there, sipping a drink like nothing'd happened, and the gun...it was on the table next to the chair."

Oh, my God, Seth, do you think it was Tess that shot him?"

He shrugged. "She said that Gilly did it, but she was just sitting there like she didn't care, and there was blood everywhere, and…and Dub's eyes were all bugged out." At this Seth closed his eyes tightly. "Dub was an okay little shit. They didn't have to kill him."

"What happened next?"

"I left."

"Did anyone call the police, Seth?"

"I didn't. I told Tess that she should, but she said she didn't wanna do it then, that she'd call 'em in the morning, and then she got up and fixed herself another drink, and that's when I left. I came straight here, Gwen. I'm sorry, but I didn't know where else to go."

She put her hand on his. "It's okay, Seth, but we have to call the police now. It can't wait till morning."

He nodded.

"And we have to call Ron Chrome too."

Seth looked up with new fear in his eyes. "Do we have to?"

"Of course. Like it or not, this is an agency matter."

"But…but I'll lose my job."

She sighed. "That's not for certain, Seth, but in any event, we have to call Ron. Tess is our client, and her brother was just shot dead in her house."

"No. That's not what happened."

Gwen shook her head with disbelief. "What do you mean, that's not what happened? What'd you just tell me? Is Dub dead or not?"

Once more, he looked away. "Yeah, he's dead, but he wasn't her brother. That's what all the fighting was about. That was the awful thing. Dub was Tess's boy."

It took a moment for Seth's words to sink in. "Dub was Tess's son?"

Seth nodded. "And Gilly was the dad."

"Aw, Jesus, Seth."

CHAPTER 26

▼

Howard Cronk looked on from the side as Senator Hester Cronk, preparing to speak, bowed her head for a moment of prayer. She was standing in the back of the Cronk Plumbing and Heating pickup, her hands resting in the wooden lectern Howard had built for just this purpose. Behind her, Scottish Jesus stood lashed in place, ready to lend credence to Hester's words. Using the pickup in this way was a standard tactic for the senator, a go-anywhere dais and an instant venue from which she could campaign in blitzkrieg-like fashion. There was no need to hire a hall or make other costly and time-consuming arrangements: just climb in the pickup and take the fight to the enemy before he knew what hit him. It was a tactic that had served Hester well over the years, a tactic that endeared her to the people and distanced her from the bosses. She had used it to win elections to the school board and the state senate, and now she was using it to rally the faithful in a time of moral crisis, though Howard had to concede that all of Hester's campaigns involved some sort of moral crisis.

And now as Howard looked over the crowd, he also had to concede that Hester had pulled it off again. There were as least two hundred people gathered in the park to hear her speak, and more importantly, crews from three Twin Cities TV stations were also on hand, and Hester had managed it all in a very short time. The fight at the Legion Club had taken place only a few hours earlier, and she'd had her first meeting with H. Landon Beard only that morning, yet here she was, ready to fight. True, the turn-

out was helped by the community ice cream social that was already scheduled for the park that evening, but Hester had no qualms about
piggybacking on another event. Besides, the TV crews and reporters
weren't there to eat ice cream; they were there to cover Hester's rally, and
that was all Hester's doing.

She had harangued the governor's office until the governor finally spoke
with her on the phone. An hour later, during a press briefing on his budget, the governor expressed vague concern over continuing events in
Hayesboro relating to the Sphinx crash. It wasn't much, but it was enough
to kindle media interest. Then too, Hester unleashed her allies in the
clergy, those rightly troubled by rampant moral decay, and they called TV
stations and newspapers to demand that light be shown on the gathering
darkness in Hayesboro. It had all worked, the media was there, and Hester
had the stage she wanted.

It wasn't what Howard had wanted though. He had hoped that he and
Hester might actually spend a quiet night at home. There were two thick,
well-marbled steaks in the refrigerator—Howard had picked them out
himself—and he had planned to grill them for dinner. There was also a
bottle of white wine in the refrigerator—the kind Hester liked—and
Howard's plan called for a nice, quiet dinner at the very least and, if he
could get enough of the wine into Hester, maybe something more. But
instead, Hester and Howard and Scottish Jesus were in the park, preparing
to do God's work. Hopes for steak and wine and nooky were rapidly dim-
ming.

Hester finished her prayer and raised her head and gazed silently for
several moments as a tense hush fell over the crowd. Then she raised the
microphone—the pickup had a portable sound system—to her lips.

"Satan has come to Hayesboro!"

Audible gasps sounded from the crowd, and Hester paused to let her
words sink in.

"People, you know that I never sugar-coat anything for political gain,
and I won't sugar-coat tonight. You also know that I always speak the
truth, no matter how troubling it might be. Well, the news I have for you
is very troubling indeed, but if we truly care about family values and our

children's welfare, if we cherish our God-fearing way of life, then we must come together and face this evil now descending on our community."

Hester paused once more, and when she spoke again, her voice was brisk and businesslike. "Here are the facts. One, last week, Sphinx, a godless corruptor of our youth, crashed his plane into a barn out at Gabriel Cox's farm. Why was he flying out this way? What were his plans? What caused the crash? We don't know the answers yet; the National Transportation Safety Board is still investigating. But some would have us believe it was all coincidence. Coincidence? I don't think so. Sphinx's tawdry life was the embodiment of evil, and last week, someone or something aimed that evil at us, and all this talk of coincidence is just an attempt to get us to lower our guard."

Hester nodded knowingly, inducing scattered nods of agreement among the crowd. "Fact number two: in the hours following his death, depraved hordes of Sphinx's followers swarmed over our town and the countryside, rioting and clogging roads and defying authority and damaging property. More coincidence?"

Cries of "No" sounded from the crowd. The people remembered. "Fact number three: just days after the crash, a satanic cult set up shop out at the Cox farm. You've all heard the rumors. Well, I'm here to tell you that they're true and also to tell you that this is no coincidence, either. This is a chain of evil, people, one which has now been verified by reliable and independent sources."

Hester paused as an uneasy murmur rippled through the crowd, and then she pointed to where H. Landon Beard was standing. "Raise your hand, Mr. Beard." Beard did so with a smug smile, and Hester continued. "H. Landon Beard is a respected attorney from Minneapolis and a trusted member of my campaign staff. He has recently been to the Cox farm on two different occasions. He has seen the cult firsthand. He has witnessed their satanic rituals. He has seen them chanting around strange fires. He has heard their prayers to the devil."

The crowd's murmur grew louder, and Hester pointed again. "Raise your hand, Slade Walters." Near the edge of the crowd, Slade Walters raised his hand. The entire right side of his face was bandaged.

Humph, thought Howard. There'd been no bandage an hour earlier when Walters appeared with Beard at the Cronk house for a meeting with Hester.

"You all know Slade. He's our neighbor. He's also neighbor to the Cox farm, living just a mile away. Two nights ago, he was on his way home, minding his own business, when he was attacked by a dozen or more Satanists. He fought them and managed to escape. Mr. Walters is a professional man, a pilot, a man trained to make quick and accurate observations, and he now corroborates Mr. Beard's accounts of the cult."

Hester paused again, allowing the crowd to gather itself around the idea of Slade Walters as a trained professional. It took a moment or two, but eventually, a few heads nodded in agreement.

"Fact number four: the Satanists are becoming bolder by the day. They have broadened their attacks. This very afternoon, they attacked and injured Mr. Walters at the Hayesboro Legion Club."

Another murmur of dismay.

"People, this is only the beginning. The Satanists will not stop; their evil cannot be avoided by sticking our heads in the sand. We have no choice here. We must act!"

Shouts of approval sounded from the crowd.

"But I have good news for you tonight. We are not alone in our struggle. Help is coming. I personally spoke with the governor, and he shares my deep concern, and I am confident that he will do what he can to help, whether it be additional law enforcement personnel or, if need be, the National Guard. Still, people, the primary responsibility to act rests with us. This is our home. It's about our values and our children's future. We are the front line, and the enemy is no less than Satan!"

Cheers rose from the crowd, and a woman near the front called out, "What can we do, Senator? We want to help, but how?"

"Good question," said Hester. "For starters, we can all pray, pray that God will give us the strength and will to meet this test. And we should all be vigilant too. Be aware of strangers, and don't hesitate to sound the alarm if something seems amiss. It's important that everyone be aware. Talk to your neighbors. Talk to your friends. Talk to the mayor and the city council and the police. They need to step up and join the fight, and we should demand that they do it. I will continue to work with the governor at the state level, and I will also work with local officials. I believe that God has called me to lead, and I will not refuse his call, but I need your help. I need for you to join hands with me in this fight against evil!"

The crowd cheered again as Hester reached back and placed her hand where Scottish Jesus' hand was nailed to the cross, bowing her head for a moment of prayer, and then she raised her hands for quiet. "Thank you all for coming tonight, and I especially want to thank the media. Your role is vital, and though I'm sure you have many questions, I'm also sure that you understand that I can't answer them at this time for reasons of security. We will, however, keep you informed with timely news releases. Again, thanks to everyone, and rest assured that we will do all we can, that we will work hard and long, beginning this very night."

Shit, thought Howard, so much for any steak and wine that night. Or anything else for that matter.

✳   ✳   ✳   ✳

As Senator Cronk concluded her remarks, Tanner Mills looked on from across the street in Gwen Todd's living room. It was dusk now, and the unlit room was dark. As Tanner watched, Gwen came and stood beside him.

"I really oughta be over there covering this," he said.

Gwen chuckled. "You'd be well advised to cover yourself first."

Tanner chuckled too. She was right, of course; he was naked, as was she.

He had arrived at her house, per their agreement, at six o'clock sharp. Gwen had been held up at the library, and she'd just gotten home, so she gave Tanner a beer and sat him down to watch the news on TV while she showered. By the time she was dressed, Tanner had helped himself to another beer, so she poured herself a glass of wine and joined him. The news ended, and she asked where he wanted to dine that night. Tanner was indifferent. Gwen's house was fine for now, he said. He preferred its ambience to that of Ted's Tavern. They talked. They talked about Gabby Cox and Sphinx and fights at the Legion Club and small towns. Tanner had another beer, and Gwen had another glass of wine, and their talk turned briefly to politics and then to theater—he surprised her with an appetite for Ibsen—and then their talk gave way to kissing and embracing. Gwen thought to protest as she had the night before but then chose not to, and soon, clothing was being loosened and then scattered on the floor. Eventually, they moved on to Gwen's bed, where they had just achieved simultaneous orgasms when an amplified voice crackled though the open bedroom window.

"Satan has come to Hayesboro!"

Tanner was still on top of her, and his eyes widened with mock surprise. "Shit! How'd they find out I was here?"

Gwen laughed. "I knew you were a horny sort, but this gives it a whole new meaning."

He rolled off her as the amplified voice sounded through the window again. "Who the hell is that?" he asked.

"If I were betting, I'd say it was Hester Cronk."

"Of course." He nodded. "I recognize the voice now. I've heard it often enough at the capitol, just never under these circumstances." He reached over and rested his hand on her hip. "And now that I think about it, having Senator Cronk's fire and brimstone pumped into the bedroom is a little too much of a Big Brother thing. Scary, huh?"

"Yes, too scary."

He listened for a moment or two longer before climbing from bed. "I gotta see this."

As the senator concluded her remarks a few minutes later, Gwen joined him in the living room, where she made her suggestion that he cover himself before covering the rally, and after due consideration, he decided against covering anything.

"Cover-ups are an anathema to dedicated members of the press," he explained. Then he chuckled. "But you gotta admit, this makes for some damn crazy politics: Hester Cronk and your pal, Slade Walters, and that

H. Landon fellow. Isn't he the ambulance chaser who was in the bar with Slade?"

Gwen nodded.

"Talk about your strange bedfellows."

Gwen shrugged. "Any alliance that does God's work is holy. As a dedicated member of the press, you should understand that, Tanner."

Now he shrugged. "What's with the cross thing she's got in the pickup with her?"

"That's Hester's crucifix. She always campaigns with it. More proof of a holy alliance."

"Yeah, now that you mention it, I've heard about that." He smiled, thought for a moment, and slipped his arm around her. "So what do you suppose the good senator would have to say about the town librarian dallying with Satan?"

"I think that it's none of the good senator's business," she said. "Now what about dinner?"

"Later." He pulled her closer.

She slid her arms around his waist. "We could eat here, I suppose. I could scramble some eggs."

"Yeah." He kissed her. "Scrambled eggs. Later."

CHAPTER 27

▼

L. R. Todd eased his pickup onto the shoulder of the highway at Hayes-boro's city limits and came to a stop. He sat there for a full minute, his hands still on the steering wheel, his dark, bushy eyebrows knitted, but try as he did, he couldn't remember why he'd driven to town. Was it something at the grocery store? He checked his shirt pocket to see if he'd made a list. No list, but that didn't mean that groceries weren't his mission. If only he could remember. Perhaps he'd come to town to see Gwen. That seemed unlikely, though. She came out to the farm each day, and he rarely visited her house in town. He disliked her house. It was too hemmed in by the neighboring houses. Besides, if he went to Gwen's house, she would only get angry. More and more, she discouraged him from driving, and recently, she'd suggested that the day was coming when he would no longer be able to drive at all. She already insisted that he not drive at night. It was dark now, and if he drove to Gwen's house, she would only get angry and lecture him. No, L. R. was fairly certain he hadn't come to town to see his daughter.

His thoughts returned to groceries, but after another full minute, he still couldn't think of any item needed in his refrigerator or pantry. Perhaps he should just go to the store, he thought, and once there, he might remember, and if he didn't remember, he might at least see something to whet his appetite. It seemed a waste to drive to the edge of town and then turn around and go home empty-handed just because he couldn't remember why he'd come in the first place. Then L. R. noticed the gas gauge. It read less than a quarter full. The co-op station where he bought his gas was just up the road, and suddenly, a full tank of gas seemed like a good reason to come to town. It might even be the reason he had.

L. R. pulled in at the self-serve island, and while his tank was filling, he methodically checked the oil and washed the windshield. Take care of your machinery. That he would never forget. Taking care of machinery was like breathing. He'd done it all his life, and he didn't have to think about it. The pump clicked off, and he replaced the nozzle. Then he stared at the pump. The cost of his tank of gas was displayed there somewhere, but there were several displays of numbers and he couldn't distinguish one from the others. He shrugged. He didn't have to understand the jumble of numbers. That was Dave's job.

Dave Morgan had worked at the co-op station for twenty-five years, since the days when they had only full service. Now there was only one full-service pump, and hardly anyone used it, so Dave spent most of his time inside at the register. He didn't have to—he was the manager now, and other employees could run the register—but Dave liked it there. It was the focal point of the whole operation. The customers funneled to it, and with them came news and gossip. Dave received the news and gossip wholesale, and then he added a markup in the form of his own opinions and retailed it back out along with the gas and cigarettes and candy bars. It had been a slow night, and when L. R. Todd came in to pay for his gas, Dave was ready at the register, standing beneath the racks of cigarettes with his best co-op smile.

"How they hanging, L. R.?"

L. R. gave Dave an oblique glance as he reached for his wallet. "Okay, I reckon. How much I owe you?"

"Twenty-eight ninety-five'll do her."

"Fucking Arabs." L. R. said this whenever he bought gas, no matter the price, and Dave had expected it.

"You got that right, L. R. Them goddamn Arabs take a dollar for every dime the co-op gets. It ain't right, and somebody oughta do something about it, but nobody ever does. The real problem's them goddamn oil companies. They're all in cahoots with them Arabs. Hell, L. R., you oughta be president of some oil company. You'd set things straight, alright."

L. R. grunted and slowly pulled two twenties from his wallet. He stared at the bills in his hand for a moment, his eyebrows knitted in attempted math, then he shrugged and dropped the money on the counter.

Dave grabbed the money and rang up the register. "You heard about the goings-on out to Gabby Cox's place?"

L. R. puzzled a moment, and then a synapse fired in his brain. Gabby Cox was his neighbor. Then another synapse fired, and L. R. said, "His barn burnt."

"Hell, L. R., that's ancient history. I'm talking news here. I'm talking about that *say*tanic cult that's set up shop out there."

L. R.'s eyebrows knitted again, but nary a synapse fired. He took a stab. "City folks?"

Dave shrugged. "Yeah, I reckon. We don't train no *Say*tanists out here in our schools and churches."

"Goddamn city folks." L. R. got things sorted that far.

"Word is, they got women out there too." Dave lowered his voice. "They say a *Say*tanist woman'll do things that'd make a whore blush."

L. R. stared at Dave. He had no idea what the man was talking about. He picked up his change from the counter and turned to leave, but Dave had more news to deliver. He leaned across the counter and lowered voice even more. "I hear there's a bunch of boys getting lathered up over to the Legion Club. I hear they might just take a little drive out to Gabby's tonight."

L. R. picked up on this. Gabby was his neighbor, and folks driving around the neighborhood at night troubled him, even if they were just lathered-up boys from the Legion Club. Then a synapse fired again, and L. R. finally saw the real danger here. "There's city folks staying at Gabby's?"

"That's what I've been telling you, L. R. You ain't been listening. It's a *say*tanic cult."

Synapses began firing in L. R.'s brain, one after another, and "satanic cult" linked directly to "sweet corn" in the maze-like passages of L. R.'s mind. "I gotta go home. They'll be in my sweet corn for sure, if they ain't already."

This unexpected segue left Dave momentarily speechless, and then he gave a short laugh. "You think them *Say*tanists are after your sweet corn? That's a good one, L.R. Word is, they got bigger things in mind."

L. R. ignored Dave. He was headed for the door. He had to get home. There was no time to waste.

CHAPTER 28

▼

Gabby sat alone on his porch, his mood dark as the night sky. His disposition had first soured that afternoon, with Gwen Todd bringing that pushy reporter out to the farm. Ever since Sphinx had crashed into his life, Gabby had come to hate anyone having anything to do with the media, but there was an added layer to his dislike for Tanner Mills. Mills had claimed that he'd just met Gwen, that she was only helping him because of her friendship with Gabby, but Gabby suspected more. Mills was glib—words came quickly and easily—and Gwen was the same way. They were alike and seemed at ease together, and that bothered Gabby. He was far from glib, so far that it seemed as if Gwen and Tanner spoke a common language that he didn't understand, and he imagined them talking about him and laughing.

Gabby's mood grew darker when Jack Sand and Kevin Calm came back from town with reports of Slade Walters' attack and with Jack's right eye swollen shut and turning a merry mottle of black and blue. Teal Osborne and Meredith Towne reacted with fear and confusion.

"Why?" they demanded. They'd only come to this place to honor and grieve their fallen idol. They meant harm to no one. Why all this hostility? What'd they done?

Gabby had no answers, and the girls then concluded that it was time to go back to New York, that they should leave that very night. Kevin agreed, but Jack dug in his heels. He wasn't about to skulk off into the night as if he were afraid of someone. They would leave the next morning, in full light of day, taking their own sweet time, and to hell with Slade Walters and his ilk.

Now, as Gabby sat on his porch, his mood grew still darker with the irony that the Shriners leaving was a further invasion of his privacy. Slade Walters and that damn lawyer Beard and all those busybodies in town had no business saying who could visit at Gabby's farm and who couldn't, but in effect that's just what they were doing. They were running the Shriners off; they were exerting control over his land—and that made Gabby mad. Besides, he'd come to like the Shriners. Oh, they were young and had some funny ideas and did some goofy things, but Gabby liked them anyway, and he sensed that they liked him too. And now he wondered who'd liked whom first, as if one had led to the other, but he couldn't decide, and then he decided that it didn't matter. For a shy man, just being liked was enough. And now his friends were leaving.

A door banged across the yard where the Shriners' camper was parked, and Gabby looked up to see Jack and Teal walking toward the house. A moment later Kevin and Meredith followed, rounding the back of the trailer. They reached the porch, and Gabby saw that each carried a bottle of beer. Actually, Jack had two and he held one out to Gabby.

"Thought we'd get together for a good-bye beer," said Jack.

"Or two," said Teal.

"Or three," said Kevin.

"And we want to thank you for letting us stay here," said Meredith. "You didn't have to. We understand that, and we really appreciate it. We came to be where Sphinx died. We had no idea what we'd find—none of us had been to Minnesota before—and we found some cruel people, but the thing we'll remember most is your kindness."

Gabby felt his spirits rise, along with a lump in his throat, and he searched for words worthy of Meredith's, but as usual, none came, so he simply took the beer from Jack's extended hand and said, "Thanks." There followed an awkward moment with Gabby sitting in his rocker and the Shriners standing around him until Gabby managed, "Won't you sit a spell?"

The Shriners sat on the porch floor, leaning back against the railing, as they had two nights earlier, but this night didn't feel like a party. The conversation was subdued and limited to travel subjects like the best routes to New York and the state of the camper's tires. Jack fetched another round of beer, but the mood remained quiet, and no one so much as mentioned pot. After a bit, the conversation ended altogether, lapsing into a comfortable silence. Several minutes passed before Teal spoke.

"The sky's so clear, and the stars are so bright," she said, her head tilted back against the rail as she stared up into the night sky. "Do you suppose Sphinx is, like, up there? Do you suppose he's a star now, like, shining down for all the world to see?"

Teal's question was met with silence, and after a moment, she answered it herself. "Well, I think he is. I think he's a star now, and I don't mean just a rock star, but a real star in the heavens." She began humming softly, and the others recognized Sphinx's signature song. Teal went on to sing, "Baby, baby, come ride my cloud. We'll slip the Earth and its smothering shroud."

Now Meredith looked skyward. "You may be right, Teal. Who knows? There's so much we don't know, but that's the thing about the spirit. Something can be right there, surrounding you, and your senses'll be completely unaware of it, but your spirit'll know. It's like a sixth sense, and if you trust your spirit, you'll feel so much more than you can ever touch or hear or see."

"Yeah," said Teal, "I feel it. Sphinx is, like, a star, and so is Sparkle. She's a smaller star, and she's next to Sphinx, and together they're, like, a new constellation."

Silence again as all heads tilted skyward, searching for a new constellation, and then Teal turned to Gabby. "You were the only one here when Sphinx and Sparkle died. You were the only witness. That makes you, like, very special."

Gabby shrugged.

"Tell us something that no one else knows," said Teal, leaning toward Gabby. "Tell us a special thing that hasn't been in the news, a special thing we can, like, keep in our hearts."

Teal's request startled Gabby, but he realized how badly he wanted to honor it, how badly he wanted to give them something that would find a place in their hearts, a place not so much for Sphinx and Sparkle, but for Gabby Cox. He searched his memory. He closed his eyes and fixed his mind's eye on that day, but nothing worthy came.

"It's all been said, I reckon." He shook his head. "The TV people and the newspaper people—they said it all about every way it can be said."

"It doesn't have to be a big thing," said Teal. "It doesn't have to be, like, newsworthy. Just some little thing you might've noticed."

Gabby thought again, and then it came to him in a flash, his gift to the Shriners. "They were naked," he blurted.

Gabby's gift met stunned silence, and he felt his face redden with the fear that his gift was horribly inappropriate.

Then Jack spoke. "Wow!"

"Yeah, like, wow!" echoed Teal.

"That's so beautiful," said Meredith. "It's…it's poetry, that's what it is. Flying naked is a poem about love and freedom. It's just beautiful."

Gabby didn't see the poetry in flying naked, but then he rarely saw the poetry in anything, and he was mostly just relieved that his gift had been well received. For a moment, it had seemed like a terrible blunder.

"So…so did you actually see them?" The question was Kevin's.

Gabby shook his head. He wouldn't taint his gift with a lie. "Sam Stack, the county sheriff—he was the first one out here that day. He saw 'em. He was the one that told me." Gabby paused. "And that fed told me I wasn't supposed to tell anyone, but to hell with him. I ain't gonna blab it all over, but you're such big fans and all, I figured it's okay if you know."

"Thank you, oh, thank you, Gabby," said Teal.

"And no one else knows?" said Meredith.

Gabby wanted to shake his head, but that would've been a lie too. "Gwen Todd knows. I told her."

"That's good," said Meredith. "Gwen's your friend, and she was a friend to us too. It's good that she knows."

"Yeah," said Teal. "I'm, like, glad you told her too, but mostly I'm just glad you told us. It makes Sphinx closer somehow, like I could stretch my arm out and touch his star."

Teal extended her arm skyward, toward approximately the spot where at just that moment a star exploded, raining fire across the sky.

Teal gasped. "Sphinx!"

Another star exploded, and then another, and only then did three thunderous bangs reach their ears.

"Holy shit!" said Jack.

"What the hell?" said Gabby, rising from his chair as a new sound, the sound of honking horns, blared through the night. They looked up the driveway to the county road, where a half dozen pickups were parked, illuminated in their own headlights, with a dozen or so men waving their arms and yelling.

"What the hell?" repeated Gabby as a new set of lights appeared behind the pickups, a single pair of headlights beneath flashing lights of red and blue. Almost immediately, the honking and yelling stopped, and in the ensuing quiet, Gabby and the Shriners stared out toward the road, wondering aloud what was transpiring out among the headlights. Their wondering lasted only a minute, and then one by one, the pickups rolled down the road, red taillights fading into billows of dust. A minute later, Sam Stack's car pulled into the yard, the flashing lights now off. Sam climbed from the car and walked toward Gabby and the Shriners on the porch.

"Evening, Gabby, folks," he said with a casual nod as if it were just a friendly visit.

"What the hell was that about, Sam?" demanded Gabby.

Sam looked out toward the road as the last set of taillights disappeared. "That was just some boys that got kinda liquored up at the Legion and decided to come out here and give you a little Fourth of July show."

"They're kinda late, ain't they? The Fourth was damn near a month ago."

Sam shrugged. "Like I said, they were liquored up a bit."

"Well, why didn't you arrest 'em for drunk driving then?"

"Don't reckon they were that liquored up. Gordy Cromer had some Roman candles left over from the Fourth, and they were just out for a little fun." Sam paused and glanced at the Shriners. "Besides, you know how people in town've been talking about your visitors here. Gordy and the boys shouldn't come as much of a surprise."

Gabby bristled. "Surprise got nothing to do with it, Sam. It's my goddamn land. They got no right coming out here in the middle of the night, raising hell and shooting off fireworks. You shoulda arrested 'em for that."

"For celebrating the Fourth late?"

"No, damn it! For trespassing."

"Well, Gabby, technically they didn't trespass. They stayed on the road, so—"

"Goddamn it, Sam, don't give me that bullshit. Who knows what they might've done if you hadn't come along?"

"Now settle down, Gabby. I got wind of what they were up to and followed 'em out here just in case things got outta hand, and now those boys are heading home where they belong. Their fun's done for the night, so don't get yourself all worked up."

Gabby started to speak, but Sam raised his hand, cutting him off. "Look, Gabby, here's the thing. Maybe those boys tonight were just out for fun, and maybe they weren't, but next time, I'm pretty sure it won't be for fun, and there *is* gonna be a next time. People are getting worked up. Hester Cronk's been stirring the pot as only she can do, and like I told you the other day, this'll all go away just as soon as your friends here get on down the road." Sam smiled and nodded at the Shriners. "Nothing personal, folks."

"But they ain't done nothing," said Gabby. "And they got a right to some protection from the law."

"Yes, they do," Sam agreed, "and they'll get it, but that doesn't guarantee that somebody won't get hurt anyway."

"We're leaving tomorrow," said Jack Sand.

Sam looked at him. "I'm glad to hear that, son. I truly am. You're doing the smart thing. I hope you've had a nice visit, but leaving's the smart thing to do."

Teal broke in. "What about that jerk Walters? He, like, assaulted Jack for no reason at all. Just look at his eye! Are you gonna arrest him?"

Sam considered Teal for a moment, and when he spoke, there was a softness, almost a sadness, in his voice. "Now that's just what I've been talking about here. You don't think Slade had reason to do what he did, and frankly, neither do I, but just the fact that you folks are here is reason enough for lots of folks."

"That ain't right," said Gabby.

Sam and the Shriners nodded their agreement.

CHAPTER 29

▼

It was past midnight when Gabby reached Hayesboro's city limits. No one was about, the streets were empty, and that emptiness sapped his confidence. He pulled to the side of the road, where he sat behind the wheel of his pickup for a long minute, fighting the urge to abandon his midnight mission, to turn around and go home. Then he steeled his resolve. His mission was daunting, but the prospect of turning back and never again finding the confidence he'd found that night was more daunting. It'd been an eventful night, but he was determined to see one more event through, and with that determination his sense of peace returned.

His peaceful mood surprised him in a way. Earlier, after the business with the fireworks, he'd been filled with rage at yet another intrusion into his privacy, and before that, his mood had been dark and sullen, but all that had changed. After Sam Stack left, Gabby and the Shriners settled on the porch for another round of beer, and the Shriners' company and friendship quickly dulled the edge of Gabby's anger. Then, with yet another round and more pleasant conversation came the surprising peacefulness.

When the Shriners finally said goodnight and walked slowly to their camper, wistfulness leaked into Gabby's stew of emotions, but the peacefulness lingered on, and he sat alone on the porch, pondering his unfamiliar feelings. After nearly an hour, he came to the remarkable conclusion that his feelings were unfamiliar only because he, with his shell of shyness, had held them at bay. He had acquaintances, but he'd never had real friends. He had never allowed himself the luxury, and he realized this now only because of how quickly and deeply friendship had rooted between him and the Shriners over the past emotion-filled days. They had reached out to him, and in turn, he had opened himself to their touch, and then surprisingly, he had reached back. He recalled with a smile his gift to them of Sphinx and Sparkle's nakedness. It was a small thing really, a bit of intimate knowledge shared between friends, but it had given them joy, and Gabby found joy in that. There had been so little sharing and joy in his life, and now came a longing for more of it, and with that longing, his thoughts turned to Gwen Todd.

Now, as he drove the quiet streets of Hayesboro, he replayed the train of thought that had come to him on the porch. He had long wanted to push his correct library relationship with Gwen to something beyond, to something real, to something warm and intimate, but he'd always been too shy, too afraid of being found unworthy. Then Sphinx crashed into his life, and for days that seemed to have destroyed much more than a barn, but now Gabby wasn't so sure. Perhaps something good was rising from the ashes of that barn. If Sphinx hadn't entered Gabby's life, then surely the Shriners wouldn't have either, and the Shriners were a good thing. He knew that now. They had shown him what was possible beyond his shyness. Then there was Gwen. In the three years before Sphinx, she had visited Gabby's farm no more than twice—and then only for neighborly reasons. Now in the last week, she'd been to the farm three times, and those visits had had a different feel to them. They had sat on his porch and talked as they never had in the library. They had partied with the Shriners, and recalling that now led Gabby to believe that Sphinx had started a chain of events, events that were meant to be, and maybe, just maybe, Gwen was also meant to be. He had only to reach out and open himself to another's touch, as the Shriners had taught him to do.

The hour was all wrong—he understood that—but he also knew that sleep was impossible that night, and he found himself in his pickup, heading for town, hoping desperately that Gwen would still be awake. He had to act while he still had the nerve. He didn't know what he would say; he only trusted that if it were truly meant to be, then words would come.

He turned onto her street and drove several blocks until he came to the park, and when Gwen's house came into view and he saw light in the windows, his heart leaped. She was awake.

He coasted to a stop and sat for a moment studying the car parked on the street in front of him. It wasn't Gwen's car, but still, it looked familiar, and then it came to him with an awful jolt. The car had been at his farm that afternoon. It was that reporter's car. He looked at the house, at the light shining through the windows, and imagined Gwen and Tanner Mills together, and suddenly, he felt like a great fool. It wasn't meant to be. He shifted the truck into gear and drove slowly into the night.

∗   ∗   ∗   ∗

Gwen Todd lay in her bed, listening to Tanner Mills' soft snores, and wondered if she should rouse him and send him back to his motel or let him sleep the night. Pale light from the living room came through the bedroom doorway, and she thought that she should at least get up and turn off the lights. Then she decided to do nothing a bit longer. A fresh summer breeze wafted through the open window, and it was pleasant lying there in the semidarkness with a sleeping man beside her. She wasn't at all sleepy. Too many thoughts filled her head for sleep, thoughts of rock stars and bachelor farmers and zealous politicians and newspaper reporters. It was a strange and unlikely chemistry indeed. Earlier, over scrambled eggs and wine, she and Tanner had talked about that chemistry, and she had placed most of the blame for it on Sphinx. Tanner had laughed. Sphinx might have started it, he'd said, but Minnesota and Hayesboro deserved a good share of the blame for what had followed. And now as Gwen recalled Tanner's remark, it called to mind a similar remark from the past.

CHAPTER 30

▼

Ron Chrome leaned back in his chair and tented his fingers under his chin. "You're making a big mistake here, Toddy."

Gwen Todd sat across the desk from him. She started to speak but just shrugged instead.

"You're good," Chrome continued. "You've got a knack for the business, but if you leave now, you'll be throwing it all away. There ain't no second chances out here in La La Land. Lots of people don't get the first one."

Gwen had just resigned her position at the Chrome Agency, and she wasn't surprised at Chrome's reaction. She had expected it, but now, even as she looked at the pictured stars on Chrome's office walls, even as she recalled her own determination to make it in Hollywood, she was convinced that she'd made the right decision.

"I've given this a lot of thought, Ron. And I'm truly grateful for the opportunity. It's been...well, unforgettable. And that's an understatement if ever there was one. Wherever I go from here, I'll always remember my Tess Snow days."

Chrome leaned forward. "But that's the point, Toddy. Tess is history. We all gotta move on. We've got other clients, and there'll always be new blood to develop. Don't screw up your career just because Tess screwed up hers."

"Tess screwed up more than her career."

"No argument there, but that's still no reason for you to throw everything away." Chrome paused. "Look, I know you're upset, and who wouldn't be? But at the end of the day, it's just business. That's all it is, Toddy, business, so don't rush into this. Take some time off and think about it. Go back to Minnesota for a while and look at the snow or whatever the hell they do up there, but don't burn your bridges."

Gwen smiled at the irony of Chrome's suggestion that she turn to snow in Minnesota as a way of dealing with Tess Snow, but she also knew that Tess wasn't the real reason she was resigning. It wasn't Tess she was running from; it was Hollywood, a place where lives were discarded like the daily trash. Still, it'd been Tess who brought matters to a head.

The police had looked long and hard at Tess at the beginning of their investigation into the murder of Dub Snow, but forensic evidence soon turned their attention to Gilly Snow. Gilly, however, had disappeared. His pickup was found abandoned in Phoenix, but there the trail went cold, and now the manhunt had moved east, to the backwoods of the Ozark Mountains.

The police investigation had been only hours old when Ron Chrome launched a masterful salvage operation. Chrome realized from the start that suspicion would soon focus on Gilly and that the greatest threat to Tess's career was Dub's pedigree. Chrome succeeded, and the investigators went forward, firm in the belief that they were dealing with a crime between siblings and not with the tragic outcome of incest.

There was still a risk of exposure, if and when Gilly was caught, but for the time being, at least Chrome had saved Tess's career. It was Tess who didn't want to be saved. Her initial indifference to the tragedy was followed by a solid month of booze and drugs, and that was followed by a complete mental breakdown and an attempted suicide. In the end, it was Gwen, not Chrome, who saved Tess. Gwen checked on Tess each day following Dub's murder, and it was she who found Tess sprawled naked and unconscious on her bedroom floor. Tess had taken a massive drug overdose, and she was barely breathing. Later, the doctor at the hospital said that she surely would have died had she been discovered half an hour later.

Tess recovered a semblance of physical health, but her mental state had turned a permanent mush, and Chrome, as much for the agency's sake as Tess's, squirreled her away in a private and exclusive sanitarium.

Now Gwen scanned the stars on Chrome's walls again. "You took Tess's picture down."

Chrome shrugged. "It's best not to be reminded of some things."

"Somebody should remember her. She deserves that much."

"Fine, Toddy, remember her. But don't throw your career away over her. Yeah, Tess's life's a tragedy, but then she never really had a chance. She had two strikes against her from the start. Anybody would, coming from a background like hers. Think about it: a three-room shack in the woods with no electricity and a crapper out back. And it only gets worse when you factor in her loving family. Her old man was a stupid hillbilly, and her mother was a stupider one who thought her only role in life was sucking her stupid husband's dick. They were dirt poor, and the old man was a moonshiner who trusted no one, so there was damn little contact with the outside world. They kept things in the family, including sleeping arrangements, so is it any wonder Tess got so fucked up?"

Gwen stared in disbelief. "You...you knew all that when the agency took her on?"

Chrome nodded. "It's called due diligence, Toddy. The business demands it. And that's also why I always insisted that as far as the public was concerned, Tess's life started when she got to Nashville. When you think about it, it's a credit to her talent that she got that far."

Gwen and Chrome considered each other across the desk for a silent moment, and then Gwen spoke. "None of this changes my decision, Ron. You see, for me it's Hollywood that's all wrong. It's treating people like livestock and always having to manage the message that I want to get away from."

Chrome snorted. "Sure, blame Hollywood. Why not? The whole god-damn country blames it for everything. Shit happens, it's Hollywood's fault. But, Toddy, when it comes to Tess Snow, you gotta admit that Arkansas owns a bunch of that shit."

CHAPTER 31

▼

Gabby Cox stood at his kitchen window at daybreak, observing his morning routine. As usual, he was wearing only boxers and a T-shirt, and he sipped his first cup of coffee while occasionally scratching his crotch. The sun was a fat red ball squatting on the horizon, and the coral sky around it was clear. The day would start warm and dry, continuing a three-week trend, but the weatherman on the radio promised change. An approaching cold front would bring a good chance of thunderstorms that afternoon.

Rain would be good, thought Gabby. The crops were starting to show stress from the near-drought conditions, and a good rain might also wash away some of the other stress that had been building in his life. His thoughts turned to the night before, to his quixotic midnight run into Hayesboro, and now in the light of day, he felt even more a fool for having made it. His shy life had always been tinged with sadness, but a fool's life was sadder still, and when his eyes fell on the Shriners' camper, his sadness deepened. They were leaving that morning. There were no signs of life around the camper, but he expected some soon. They were anxious to get on the road, to get away from Hayesboro, and although he didn't blame them, he would miss them nonetheless.

Then, as if ordained by Gabby's thoughts, Jack Sand appeared from behind the camper, followed by Kevin Calm. The two men walked slowly along the camper's flank like pilots doing a preflight check—Kevin even kicked a tire—and when they came to the front, they raised the hood.

They really are getting an early start, thought Gabby, and he put down his coffee and started upstairs to get dressed. He didn't think they would leave without saying good-bye, but he wasn't going to give them a chance.

Thirty minutes later, he was standing in the yard with the Shriners. The camper's engine was idling, and Gabby's hands were shoved in his pockets. He was having difficulty making eye contact.

Jack held out his hand. "Thanks for everything, man. It's been, like, cool."

Gabby shook his hand and nodded, and when Kevin stepped forward, he shook his hand too. Next came Teal, and Gabby held out his hand again, but she would have none of it. She circled her arms around his neck and kissed his cheek and whispered her thank you in his ear. Meredith was shorter than Teal, so she hugged Gabby around his waist, and when she kissed him, her lips were softer on his cheek than Teal's had been.

Gabby breathed deep and summoned words to make his good-bye. "Well, if you're ever back this way, be sure to—" He stopped mid-sentence, suddenly aware of a hissing sound.

They all exchanged questioning looks as the hissing grew louder, and then they turned to the camper, where steam was now billowing from beneath the engine.

"Aw, shit," said Jack.

Half an hour later, Gabby walked from the house to the porch, where the Shriners were waiting. "I got hold of Irv at the auto parts store. He doesn't have a heater hose that'll fit your camper in stock, but since it's so early, he can have one on the noon bus."

Jack shrugged. "Coulda been worse, I guess."

*   *   *   *

Most mornings, Sam Stack got to his office by seven. It permitted him a quiet cup of coffee and time to assess reports of overnight shenanigans before the new day's problems began coming in. This morning, he was relieved to learn that there'd been no new mischief following the fireworks out at the Cox farm. Given the local mood, he'd half-expected something, but now he had reason to hope for avoiding further trouble altogether, given that Gabby's goofy visitors were leaving that morning. Sam's feet were on his desk, and he was sipping coffee and studying the Minnesota Twins' box score in the morning paper when a strident voice violated his calm.

"Sheriff, I demand that you do something about this satanic cult out at the Cox farm."

Sam looked up to find Hester Cronk framed in his doorway. Deputy Dora Dingles stood behind her. "I'm sorry, Sheriff," said Deputy Dingles. "I told her you were busy, but she just charged in anyway."

"You don't look all that busy to me," said Hester, "and frankly, I find that troubling, given this grave threat to our community."

Sam sighed and took his feet off the desk. "It's alright, Dora. I've always got time for Senator Cronk," he said, making no effort to conceal his sarcasm. "Cup of coffee, Senator?"

"No, thank you. This isn't a social call. We have serious matters to discuss."

"Can I get you a refill, Sheriff?" asked Dora.

Sam shook his head. "Not just now, Dora. The Senator and I have serious matters to discuss."

Dora glared briefly at Hester, then she turned and left. Sam nodded toward the chair across from his desk. "Have a seat, Senator."

Hester sat down. "As you know, Sheriff, I am a strong supporter of law enforcement. People such as yourself provide a vital service, and I always go to bat for you in the legislature, but frankly, I feel that you've betrayed my support with your failure to do your duty."

Sam hesitated before speaking. He was determined not to let this irritating woman get to him. "And what duty is that, Senator?"

"Why, the cult, of course. It's a clear threat to our safety. It threatens our very way of life. At the least, you should have run those people out of the county days ago."

"Actually, we don't run people outta the county anymore. Haven't for some time. If folks break the law, we arrest 'em, and if they don't break the law, we leave 'em alone. We find that works pretty well."

Hester thrust out her jaw. "Don't get insolent with me, Sheriff. I know how the law works. And I also know a threat to public safety when I see one. I understand there was another incident out at the Cox place last night. Are you going to wait until someone gets killed or they start abducting our children before you do anything?"

"Goddamn it, Senator—"

"And offensive language is no substitute for doing your duty, Sheriff."

Sam glared at her for a moment and then held up two fingers. "Two things, Senator. One, I was out at Gabby's last night, and what trouble there was, was caused by some liquored-up boys from the Legion Club, not by anybody staying out there. And two, and hear this good, Senator, there ain't no cult out there, satanic or otherwise. There're just some harmless Sphinx fans, four of 'em to be exact, camping with Gabby's permission, and they're leaving this morning."

"How do you know that?"

"They told me so."

Hester laughed. "You're awfully gullible for a law man, Sheriff."

Despite his best effort to remain calm, Sam felt his face redden with anger. "What's that supposed to mean?"

"It means that you're ignoring numerous credible reports of cult activity out there, reports that also indicate many more than four Satanists. Why, I've heard as many as a hundred, with more coming every day."

Sam shook his head wearily. "Senator, there are only four. I have no idea what their religion is, nor do I care, but I do know that there are only four. They haven't broken any laws that I know of, and they're leaving today."

Hester snorted. "So they'd have you believe. Have you searched the buildings? Why, there could be dozens hiding in the grove alone."

Sam laughed. "Good point, Senator. That grove could be just packed with Satanists and terrorists and homosexuals and politicians and you name it, but somehow, I don't think so."

"Don't be flip with me, Sheriff. I'll remind you that I'm a duly elected Minnesota state senator."

Sam nodded. "And now you're getting down to the nub here. You're a senator, alright, and this just happens to be an election year, and that's what I think this is really about."

Anger flashed in Hester's eyes. "I deeply resent your implication, Sheriff. This isn't about politics. I place public safety above politics, but since you bring it up, you'd also be well advised to bear in mind that this is an election year. The voters might not think well of your refusal to do your duty."

Sam smiled and shrugged.

"For the record, Sheriff, I'll ask you one more time. Will you do your duty and deal with this cult?"

"Yes. Just as soon as someone breaks a law or there's a legitimate threat to public safety."

Hester sniffed. "Very well, Sheriff. Don't be surprised if people take matters into their own hands." With that she got up and left.

*   *   *   *

Breakfast at Gwen Todd's house consisted of coffee, orange juice, and toast. Gwen spread strawberry jam on her toast and looked across the kitchen table to where Tanner Mills was opting for peanut butter. There was a morning-after awkwardness in the air; neither had said much since getting up, and now Gwen made an attempt at conversation.

"So have you figured out the storyline for your article?"

Tanner pondered as he chewed. "Not really. It's kinda hard to figure the storyline before the story's played out."

"What's still to play out?"

Tanner shrugged. "Lots of stuff. Sphinx's plane crash is old news—it's been written about ad nauseum—but now the real story is what we were talking about last night, all this weird-ass chemistry that the crash got started."

"For instance?"

"Well, for starters, you've got Hester Cronk on her high horse. You can't pick up a newspaper these days without finding her brand of evangelical vitriol taking aim at something. Then there's the local good ol' boy element; clowns in pickup trucks are always a good angle, especially if you're looking for evolutionary links to lower species. Then throw four slightly goofy New York kids into the mix along with a good dose of human nature. People'll take a good conspiracy theory over the facts any day. No, library lady, it ain't over. Gabby Cox's barn dance has got at least one more set to play."

Gwen chuckled. "Barn dance?"

"It's a metaphor. So shoot me; I'm a writer. And don't forget romance. A library lady oughta know that every story's got a love angle."

She chuckled again. "And what's the love angle here? Worldly reporter seduces small-town librarian?"

"Naw. Sounds too much like *The Music Man*. I think it goes more like this: Shy bachelor farmer loves library lady chastely from afar."

"Would you get off that? Gabriel and I are just friends."

"And you're in denial again. Don't you see the way the guy looks at you?"

Gwen bristled. "What's the deal, Tanner? You find your way into my bed and now on the morning after you're professing another guy's love for me. How am I supposed to feel about that?"

Tanner laughed. "Pissed, I imagine. Look, Gwen, I'm not trying to bail out of a one-night stand here. I like you, and I'd like to think we can go beyond that, but I'd feel better about us having a relationship if you weren't so blind to how Cox feels about you."

"Why should you care about how Gabriel feels?"

"I don't. I care about how you feel."

Gwen shook her head. "What I feel right now is confused."

*   *   *   *

Howard Cronk didn't like the feel of things one bit. He felt as if he were being swept along by yet another tidal wave of his wife's making. He should be used to it by now, he supposed. Over the years, Hester had pushed him in many directions he didn't want to go, but he was particularly uneasy with her current crusade. He didn't say as much, of course. Speaking out would only invite Hester's ire, and by remaining silent, he could cling to the hope of being spared a role in her plans. The others seated around the Cronk kitchen table—H. Landon Beard and Slade Walters—weren't saying much either, but they did seem a good deal more enthusiastic than Howard. As usual, Hester did most of the talking while her newly formed elite cadre listened.

"I fully expect the voters to deal with Sam Stack's spineless performance in November," Hester said now, concluding a narrative of her disappointing visit to the sheriff's office. "But obviously, this cult business can't wait until then. Something must be done now."

"What about the governor?" asked Beard. "He's got the Department of Public Safety; he's got the Bureau of Criminal Apprehension; he's got the State Patrol; and as a last resort, he's got the National Guard."

Hester pursed her lips for a thoughtful moment and then shook her head. "The governor certainly has those tools as his disposal, and I'm also quite certain that he's firmly on our side, but I don't think he can act quickly enough. It's a question of inertia. He has too many bureaucratic obstacles to deal with, and then there are the political considerations as well. No, Mr. Beard, if this cult is to be dealt with in a timely manner, we'll have to take the initiative ourselves."

Beard shook his head. "Too bad we can't get the sheriff to do his job."

Hester raised an eyebrow. "Perhaps we can, Mr. Beard. Perhaps we can."

Howard's stomach churned sourly at the thought of what was coming next.

Hester leaned forward. "If we force the issue, if we create a crisis in public safety, then Sheriff Stack will have to act. He said as much himself."

"How do we do that?" asked Beard.

"We don't. The people of Hayesboro do, rising in righteous rebellion." Hester turned to Slade Walters. "Can you organize the men who shot off the fireworks last night and perhaps a dozen or so more?"

Slade shrugged. "I 'spose. What for?"

Hester smiled. "If the people rise up and march on the cult, if there's a confrontation, then the sheriff'll have to respond."

"What if he just ignores us?" asked Beard.

"He won't dare. Not if there're enough of us. And not if there's ample media coverage." Hester nodded confidently. "Maybe the governor can't deploy his assets on short notice, but I can get the media out. I'll get to work on that right away. Mr. Beard, you and Mr. Walters start organizing the masses. The more the merrier. We march on the cult this afternoon."

Slade pounded his fist on the table, suddenly seized by religious fervor. "I'll getcha a hundred, maybe more. And I'll lead 'em in there myself."

"A hundred'll be wonderful, Mr. Walters," said Hester, "but you won't be leading them. I have a different job for you. A very special job."

Eyebrows rose around the table, but Hester offered nothing more about Slade's special job. Instead, she turned to her husband. "Howard, we'll need the crucifix mounted in the pickup again."

Howard wasn't hopeful, but he made a half-hearted attempt at getting out of it. "I'm supposed to service Bob Hatcher's furnace this afternoon."

"For heaven's sake, Howard, it's August. That furnace can wait another month. And besides, this is God's will."

The sourness in Howard's stomach churned faster. *Here we go again*, he thought.

*   *   *   *

A late lunch on Gabby's porch had been a listless affair, consumed in humid heat. Clouds were banking in the west, promising relief, but for now the still, sultry air only added weight to the Shriners' leave-taking, which had drawn on since early morning. Gabby had driven to town before lunch to get the new heater hose, and now the camper was repaired and ready to go, but the lethargy of heat and lunch slowed momentum. They had been sitting in silence for several minutes when Kevin Calm spoke.

"Looks like rain coming."

They looked to the west, to the banking clouds with darkened bellies. "We need some rain," said Gabby. "A good inch'll make the crop."

The Shriners nodded at this bit of farm wisdom, and Meredith Towne added a bit of non-farm wisdom. "It might be good for the crop, but it'll be better for us if we don't have to drive in it."

"Right." Jack Sand stood. "Time to go."

The others stood and stretched, but before they could step down off the porch, Kevin pointed out toward the road. "What's that about?"

They turned to look. Dust billowed up along the county road as a long line of vehicles sped toward them and slowed near the Cox driveway. The sound of honking horns blared through the still air.

"Kinda early for more fireworks, isn't it?" said Jack.

Gabby watched the approaching vehicles with clenched teeth. He was sick and tired of mobs, Sphinx fans or otherwise, showing up uninvited at his farm.

"Should we, like, call the sheriff?" asked Teal.

Gabby glared a moment longer before turning for the house. "Yeah, I'll call 'im. And I'm getting my shotgun too."

∗   ∗   ∗   ∗

Gwen Todd looked up from her desk to find Tanner Mills framed in her office doorway. "The righteous are rising," he said.

"Huh?"

"The righteous are rising, and they're gonna smite your pal, Cox."

"Tanner, what are you talking about?"

"Hester Cronk, of course. She's rounded up a holy posse, and as we speak, she's leading 'em out to Cox's place to smite the cult in the name of the Lord."

"Dear God, Tanner, are you sure?"

"Yep. It's all over town. I gotta get out there. It's where my story is. Wanna come along?"

Gwen hesitated only a moment. "Yes."

*   *   *   *

L. R. Todd looked out his kitchen window to the weather gathering in the west. It was going to rain, and L. R. nodded his satisfaction at this. His last planting of sweet corn needed rain, and so did L. R. The oppressive heat was adding to the anxiety that had plagued him for days now. Rain would be good. Then his eyes widened at the billows of dust near the Cox farm. Too much dust, he thought, far too much for a single vehicle. Fireworks the night before, and now another big crowd was heading his way. It was more than L. R. could take. His anxiety spiked, and two thoughts connected in his brain: City folks and sweet corn.

*   *   *   *

The righteous were led into Gabby Cox's barnyard by the Cronk Plumbing and Heating pickup. Hester's eight-foot crucifix was mounted upright in the box. The song "Onward Christian Soldiers" blared from the pickup's sound system. Hester Cronk's army followed in an assortment of pickups, along with a few SUVs, at least twenty altogether, some new and shiny, some old and rusty, many with gun racks in the rear window. Each vehicle was occupied by two or three men, mostly young, and all wearing ball caps, some with the visor forward, some with the visor aft. With the exception of Hester, the womenfolk had remained in town to await the victors. Bringing up the rear were two vans from Twin Cities TV stations. Hester had hoped for more, but she was satisfied with two. She knew the power of television.

On Gabby Cox's porch, Teal Osborne stared wide-eyed and clung to Jack Sand. Meredith Towne clung in the same manner to Kevin Calm while Gabby clutched his shotgun and glared angrily at the trespassers.

The Cronk pickup crunched to a stop in front of the house. Howard Cronk was at the wheel, Hester beside him. The other vehicles came to a stop in a random spread behind their leader like tanks arrayed for battle. Men began climbing from the vehicles, some with guns, but Hester and

Howard remained in their cab. "Onward Christian Soldiers" stopped suddenly, and a moment of eerie silence fell over the yard. Then Hester's voice crackled over the sound system.

"We've come in the name of the Lord to escort you out of our county. If you do not resist, no one will be harmed." A pause. "Where are the rest of the Satanists?"

Another pause as Gabby and the Shriners stared in disbelief. Then Hester's voice sounded again, now issuing orders to her troops. "Search the outbuildings. Search the grove. But don't fire unless you're fired upon."

Men spread out across the yard.

*   *   *   *

Gwen fretted as they drove out of town in Tanner's car. "I just hope this thing doesn't get out of hand."

Tanner snorted. "It'd be my guess that getting outta hand is exactly what the good senator has in mind."

"But why? What's to gain?"

Tanner smiled now. "It'd also be my guess that I won't be the only member of the media covering her little shindig."

Gwen stared at him, understood what he was saying, and then shook her head. "The gall of that woman. It's just amazing how Hester's political agenda always coincides so nicely with God's will."

Tanner turned off the highway and onto the graveled county road. "And why not? God's always on her side in the senate, so why not out here with her base?" He thought a moment. "But now that I mention it, that's what I don't get. Her base. Especially these good 'ol boys. They don't strike me as religious types."

"They're not. They're just narrow-minded brawlers. They'll fight anybody. Hester understands that and uses it. All in the name of the Lord."

A minute later, Tanner slowed as they approached Gabby's driveway, and the many vehicles parked in the yard came into view. "Dear God," said Gwen. "Look at them all."

Tanner glanced in the rearview mirror and saw flashing lights. "The law's right behind us."

"Good."

"Yeah, that's probably part of Hester's plan too."

Tanner parked as close to the house as he could and looked around the yard. "Am I the only person in this county who doesn't drive a pickup?"

"Chariots for the common man," said Gwen.

"Mobility for morons," said Tanner.

Gwen ignored him and climbed from the car. She hurried toward the porch, where, to her horror, Gabby stood next to the clinging Shriners, holding a shotgun. After grabbing his notebook, Tanner got out and hesitated, wondering from where best to cover the story, but then he followed Gwen. Gabby Cox didn't seem any more pleased to see Tanner than he did the mob running across his yard.

＊   ＊   ＊   ＊

Sam Stack stopped at the entrance to Gabby's driveway and keyed his radio mike. He was alone in his cruiser, but there were two deputies in each of the two cruisers behind him. "Ed, you and Larry follow me in," the sheriff said. Then he directed the deputies in the second car to block the driveway. "Nobody comes in without my okay."

Sam gave two quick whoops of his siren as he entered the yard, but it didn't have the desired effect. Men were running in every direction, many with shotguns or rifles, and most of them ignored the siren.

"Shit!" said Sam, and then he switched on the car's speaker system. A moment later, his voice crackled across the yard with all the authority he could muster. "This is the sheriff! Everybody stop right where you are! Anybody carrying a weapon put it on the ground immediately!"

Progress. Most of the men stopped. Some even put down their guns. Then all eyes turned to the Cronk Plumbing and Heating pickup, where Senator Hester Cronk had climbed into the box and now stood next to her crucifix. She raised a mike to her mouth.

"You have no authority here, Sheriff. Any authority you might've had came to you from the people, but you refused your duty, and now the people have taken that authority back for themselves."

Thunder rumbled, and Sam glanced off to the west; he had a sudden hope for torrential rain. He was quite sure that a quick soaking would take the starch out of Hester's crusaders, but he was also certain that he couldn't sit in the car and wait. Men were picking up their guns and moving again, and Hester keyed her mike to urge them on.

"Find the other Satanists! You are doing the work of the Lord! There's no greater authority than God's will!"

"Goddamn it," muttered Sam, and he climbed from the car, unholstered his pistol, and fired two shots into the air. The sharp crack of the gunshots, immediately reinforced by a loud crack of thunder, turned the momentum back to Sam, and the running men stopped again in confusion.

That's better, thought Sam, sensing a growing control of the scene, but then a shotgun blast sounded behind him, and control dissolved back to chaos. Sam whirled toward the house, where Gabby Cox stood on the porch, his just-fired shotgun extended into the air.

"Goddamn it, Gabby!" Sam yelled. "Put that gun down!"

Gabby ignored him, yelling instead at the running men. "Get the hell off my land!" Then he fired into the air again.

Men were diving for cover everywhere now. "The Satanists are shooting at us!" someone yelled.

It took another minute and the help of his two deputies for Sam to once again gain control, and then he jabbed a finger at Gabby. "Put that gun away now!"

Gabby complied to the extent of leaning the shotgun against the porch railing, so Sam turned toward the Cronk Plumbing and Heating pickup. "I don't wanna hear another peep from you over that sound system, Senator."

H. Landon Beard appeared suddenly at the side of the pickup. He wore the only coat and tie in sight. He looked completely out of place, but that didn't stop him from thrusting his jaw at Sam. "That's a violation of the senator's First Amendment rights, Sheriff, with respect to both freedom of speech and her right to worship as she chooses."

Sam took a step toward Beard. "One more word outta you, and I'll lock your ass up!"

H. Landon Beard harrumphed indignantly, but he also backed up a step and said no more.

Hester wasn't through, though. "You're the one responsible for this, Sheriff. You're the one who refused to see the evil out here. Well, just look around you. Look at the chaos."

"Hell, Senator," Sam sputtered, "if there's chaos out here, it's only because you brung it!"

"The other Satanists are hiding in the grove, Sheriff. I'm certain of it."

Sam turned away in disgust, only to find himself staring into the lens of a shoulder-mounted video camera. "Get the hell back," he snarled at the cameraman.

The cameraman ignored him and rolled tape. He had ignored Twin Cities police for years, and some yokel sheriff wasn't about to stop him now.

Sam was taking a menacing step toward the camera when one of his deputies called out. "Sam, someone's driving in across the field."

Sam looked out across the stubble of corn that a mob of Sphinx fans had trampled only days earlier. "Aw, shit," he said. Once more, his road-block at the end of Gabby's driveway was being easily skirted like some Maginot Line, this time by a pickup that was bouncing in across the field.

Hester Cronk had been growing increasingly desperate over her army's failure to discover cult members in appreciable numbers, and now she cried out in triumph. "It's a Satanist!"

Then Gwen Todd gasped from the porch. "Oh, my god, it's Dad!"

The TV cameraman swung to tape the arriving Satanist as L. R. Todd bounced into the yard, drove behind the other pickups, and crunched to a stop near the charred ruins of the barn. When he climbed from the cab, Gwen gasped again. L. R.'s eyes, always wild beneath his bushy black eyebrows, now had the look of complete lunacy. And worse yet, he was brandishing a shotgun as he bellowed, "Stay the hell outta my sweet corn!"

Lightning flashed across the darkening sky behind L. R., and a sudden gust of wind tousled his hair wildly to the crack of thunder.

Tanner Mills looked at Gwen. "Jesus! You never told me your old man was King Lear."

Gwen ignored him and ran toward her father. Tanner followed, as did Gabby, with shotgun in hand once more. Sam Stack was moving in the same direction, yelling for everyone to stay back, and when he was twenty feet from L. R., he stopped and held out his arms. Gwen and Tanner and Gabby stopped beside him.

"Put the gun down, L. R.," Sam ordered.

"Please, Dad," Gwen pleaded, "put the gun down."

L. R. looked at them without a hint of recognition in his wild eyes. He was holding the gun in his right hand, and now he raised it up and out as if he were Moses, preparing to part the Red Sea. Lightning flashed again, followed quickly by a clap of thunder.

"Please, Dad," said Gwen. "Please!"

L. R. stood like a statue, and Sam Stack took a step closer. "Easy, L. R." Another step. "Nice and easy now."

A tense hush filled the yard between claps of thunder as all eyes watched the sheriff edge toward the madman. Then came a new sound, faintly at first, but it quickly grew, and all heads turned in its direction. Then, just as the sound became a recognizable roar, an airplane appeared, coming in low over the grove.

"Sphinx!" cried Teal Osborne. "He's come back!"

"Like hell," yelled Gabby. "That's Slade Walters in his goddamn crop duster."

Heads ducked as the plane passed close overhead with a deafening roar and then climbed into a banking turn.

"Only a fucking fool'd fly into weather like this," said Tanner.

Sam nodded. "That'd be Slade. A world-class fucking fool."

Slade turned his plane for another run, and Hester Cronk, defying the sheriff's order, keyed her mike. "Listen to me, people! This is a moment of triumph. Just days ago, an airplane from hell crashed into that barn and let loose evil among us. But today, we have a different plane. Today, there will be no crash—because this is a flight of redemption. Slade Walters is flying for Jesus!"

Hester's army cheered as they watched Slade come in low over the grove again. L. R. Todd watched too, but he didn't cheer. It seemed to L. R. that the plane was coming directly at him, and with an instinct honed over many years, he aimed his gun.

BOOM!

In the instant following the shot, every eye was riveted on the plane, fully expecting it to veer out of control and crash, but the plane soared skyward again. L. R. had missed. In the next instant, Sam Stack tackled L. R. from behind, driving him to the ground and knocking the shotgun from his hands.

"The Lord protected Slade," Hester exalted into her mike, "and now he's coming in for another pass to the glory of God!"

Once more all eyes turned to the plane.

Sam Stack looked up from the ground, where he still had L. R. Todd pinned. "The dumb shit doesn't even know he got shot at."

Gabby was standing nearby, but the sheriff's words didn't register. His eyes were locked on the plane as another plane flashed through his brain, a plane with blonde hair showing in cockpit. Slade was coming even lower this time, and yet another vision flashed in Gabby's brain: the big cottonwood tree reaching up to knock a plane from the sky. Slade was headed directly at that tree. Gabby froze, certain Slade would hit it. But at the very last instant, Slade lifted his highly maneuverable crop duster just enough to clear the tree.

Son of a bitch, thought Gabby. *He missed it.*

A stab of lightning flashed across the sky. For the briefest instant, Slade Walters glowed brightly in the cockpit, and then the plane exploded into a ball of fire and crashed into the already burnt barn. A moment later, the clouds opened up, and torrents of rain poured down.

CHAPTER 32

▼

The Shriners' camper broke down two more times, and it took them four days to drive from Minnesota, but now they were parked at a rest stop along I-80 in eastern Pennsylvania, just two hours from home. Jack Sand and Kevin Calm stood at the front of the camper, their arms folded as they stared wordlessly beneath the open hood at the engine. Teal Osborne and Meredith Towne watched from sixty feet away, sipping sodas at a picnic table in the shade of an oak tree.

"So what's wrong with it now?" asked Teal.

Meredith shrugged. "Nothing that I know of. They just don't trust it anymore. Every time we stop, they open up the hood and stare at the engine like that. They never touch anything. They just stare. It's a guy thing, I guess. Some kinda machinery metaphysics."

"Well, I'll be glad to get home." Teal sighed. "In a way, I kinda wish we'd never gone to Minnesota."

"Really?"

"Well, yeah. I mean, it was gonna be this great spiritual journey. We were gonna connect with Sphinx and all the good stuff we felt about his music and his life but…but all we connected with was evil."

"We met some good people too, Teal. Kind people."

"Yeah, but for every good one, there were ten bad ones."

"So?" Meredith laughed. "That just puts Minnesota close to the national average."

"How can you joke about it, Mere? You're the deep one. You're, like, way more sophisticated when it comes to spirituality and God and stuff. Doesn't it bother you that God would let all this evil happen?"

Meredith shrugged. "That's not the way I see it, Teal. I don't claim to know God the way some people do, but I'm pretty sure God is good. I'm pretty sure God is love. Oh, at times, his sense of humor seems kinda strange, but the evil's not his making."

"So then do you believe in, like, Satan?"

"Naw." Meredith shook her head. "Evil's man-made, just like religion. God gives us choice, but that doesn't make him responsible for evil. He lets us make what we will of life, and too often we choose evil over good, hate over love."

Teal pondered this with a frown and turned a glum gaze back to Jack and Kevin, who were still staring at the engine. "Well, I'm not too sure about any of that stuff, but I am pretty sure that the camper's evil."

"There you go. It's man-made."

*   *   *   *

L. R. Todd stared out the window at the brick wall twenty feet away. He hated the wall. He hated being closed in. He hated not being able to look out onto his fields, and along with his hating came fear. L. R. was quite certain that the wall was moving closer each day and that soon it would crush him. He had told the nurse about the wall, but the nurse hadn't believed him. L. R. wasn't surprised. He doubted that the nurse was really a nurse. Nurses are women who dispense TLC. L. R.'s nurse was a man, a big, mean-looking one, who watched L. R. warily whenever he came into the room and never dispensed anything that resembled TLC. For that matter, L. R. doubted that the hospital was really a hospital. He'd never been in a hospital with steel mesh covering the windows. He'd never been in a hospital where they kept the doors locked so that the patients couldn't leave their rooms.

Gwen had been to see him twice, and both times, he'd asked her when he could go home—no one in the so-called hospital would tell him—but she wouldn't say, either. She just said something about getting his medication right first. She also said something about some kind of evaluation, but she couldn't say who would do the evaluating. L. R. hoped it wouldn't be his nurse. He also hoped that they'd get their medicating and evaluating done before the wall crushed him. He feared that they wouldn't. But more than anything, he feared that Gwen, his only child, was now in cahoots with the city folks.

✳   ✳   ✳   ✳

Howard Cronk wrapped Scottish Jesus in plastic and put him away with the plumbing supplies at the back of the garage. It was unusual to be storing the crucifix in August; normally, it would be in constant use between now and Election Day, but things had changed. Howard supposed that if L. R. Todd had managed to shoot Slade Walters down with his shotgun, things might now be different, but L. R. had missed. No, it'd been lightning that hit the plane, causing the fuel tank to explode, and because lightning was a weapon of choice favored by God, Hester was no longer quite so sure of God's will. Howard didn't expect Hester's uncertainty to last, but for the time being, he planned to get caught up on the plumbing and heating business. And perhaps there might even be some time for their marriage.

Howard walked from the garage into the kitchen, where he found Hester seated at the table, making notes on a legal pad. Without looking up, she said, "Pastor Sanders just called. There's a rally at church tonight. The bishop is coming to speak against same-sex marriage, and Pastor wants me to speak too."

Howard leaned against the sink and folded his arms across his chest. "We're not going."

Hester looked up, puzzled. "Well…Pastor expects a good crowd. I really should go, and you know I don't like going to these things alone."

"I said *we* are not going."

Hester frowned and stood and walked slowly toward her husband. "Am I missing something here? Am I scheduled for something else tonight?"

Howard nodded. "Yeah, dinner. I'm gonna grill those steaks in the fridge, and we're gonna drink that bottle of wine."

"But...Howard? My campaign."

"Look, Hester, you've been a senator every night for the past month. Tonight, you're gonna be a wife."

Hester blinked with surprise. "Why, Howard."

His arm circled her waist, and his hand pressed against the small of her back, drawing her close, while his other hand raised her skirt and pressed between her legs.

"Why...Howard." She pushed against his hand.

*   *   *   *

"I liked your barn dance story."

"Thank you." Tanner Mills nodded. He knew the feature he'd written about all the goofiness out in Hayesboro was good, but it was still nice to hear his editor say so. Tanner had been called into his editor's office, and now he wondered if it had been only to compliment him on his writing. That would be out of character—his editor favored sticks over carrots. *But then, why not?* thought Tanner; everything else had been going his way of late. He was out of his editor's doghouse, and more importantly, he was also out of the governor's doghouse and back on the capitol beat. That had come as a great relief, but then it'd been a relief just getting away from the sticks and back to the quick pulse and blessed anonymity of the city.

And on top of everything else, he'd come home to find his girlfriend moved back into his apartment. Their brief separation had done them good. There was electricity in their relationship again, and she hadn't said a word about commitment, though he knew it would come up eventually. And when it did...well, maybe it was time for commitment. With everything else in his life going so right, maybe it was the right time for that too.

"And Perkins upstairs liked the story too," the editor said.

"Great," said Tanner. A compliment from the managing editor never hurt.

"Perkins mentioned that maybe you oughta do feature writing full-time, that you could concentrate on these Outstate Minnesota stories, sorta be our poet from the hinterlands."

Tanner's stomach knotted. He thought he might be sick. "You...you can't be serious?"

The editor shrugged. "Doesn't matter what I think. Perkins is the boss, and it's his idea."

"Aw, Jesus, don't do this to me. I'm a political reporter, not a sob sister. And if you send me back out to the sticks, I'll go nuts."

"The sticks? I'd think a seasoned political reporter would think of them as the hustings."

"Screw the hustings! I'd rather write the fucking obits than—" Tanner stopped abruptly when he saw a glint in his editor's eye. "Are you fucking with me?"

His editor gave a "who—me?" shrug, and in the next moment, his face dissolved into a grin, and he laughed out loud. "I can't play golf anymore on account of my arthritis. I gotta get my fun somewhere."

"You son of a bitch!"

His editor laughed again. "Now get your ass back to work, and don't piss off the governor again."

*   *   *   *

Gabby Cox watched as the last truckload of blackened timbers drove from his yard, followed by another truck pulling a big backhoe on a flat-bed trailer. A concrete slab was now all that remained of the barn, and Gabby was relieved that the charred ruins were no longer there to remind him of the awful improbability of two planes crashing at the exact same spot in just a matter of days, though he wasn't likely to forget it anytime soon.

Fortunately, the aftermath of Slade Walters' crash hadn't been nearly so convulsive as Sphinx's because Slade didn't have legions of fans and also because most of the locals had always expected Slade to die young anyway. The media had played it down too, treating the second crash as a statistically interesting, but otherwise insignificant, footnote to the Sphinx drama. The bossy feds had returned, of course, but even their bureaucratic sensibilities were less strident for a fallen crop duster than they'd been for a fallen rock star.

Now it was finally cleaned up, and life could go on, though it was clear to Gabby that life would be different. He was still nagged by what had brought the rock star and his girlfriend, naked in an airplane, to his farm that day, though he was resigned to never knowing. Gwen Todd had insisted it was coincidence, nothing more, but whether it was coincidence or not, three people had died violently on Gabby's land, leaving a permanent mark that couldn't be hauled away on a truck. To Gabby's way of thinking, Sphinx and Sparkle—and even Slade—were now part of that land, and because Gabby was too, they were all kin in a sense. Gabby shuddered. It was true what they said: you could choose your friends, but not your relatives.

And Gabby was mindful that it hadn't been all turmoil and strife; there'd been good in it too. He'd made new friends, the Shriners, and although he doubted that he would ever see them again, their friendship lingered and spoke to him of other possibilities. Those possibilities crowded Gabby's thoughts as much as the plane crashes, and now that the last trace of the barn had been hauled away and his yard was orderly once more, he nodded with satisfaction and climbed into his pickup. He had one remaining task that day.

Fifteen minutes later, Gwen Todd looked up from her desk to find Gabby framed in her office doorway. She smiled. "How are you, Gabriel?"

"Okay." A pause. "They just hauled away the last of the barn. It's all cleaned up. Thought you'd like to know."

"I imagine that's a relief."

He nodded.

"Are you going to build a new one?"

He nodded again. "Just a steel building, though. Nobody builds wooden barns anymore."

"That's a shame."

"Yeah." Another pause. "How's your dad?"

Gwen shrugged. "He's okay for now. They're still working on getting his medication right. It'll be a while before anything's decided long-term, but it's not likely he'll ever live independently again. His days on the farm are over, I'm afraid."

"That's too bad."

She nodded. "Thank you for asking about him."

"Well, he was my neighbor."

They fell silent, and as the silence quickly grew uncomfortable for Gabby, he cast his eyes downward.

"Was there something else?" she asked.

"Um, I just returned a book," he said without looking up.

"Oh."

Then he looked up. "And…and I was wondering if maybe you'd, um, like to go to dinner tonight. To a restaurant, I mean."

"Dinner?"

She seemed surprised by his offer, and Gabby's stomach knotted.

"Actually," Gwen started, then she paused.

God, thought Gabby, *she's trying to think of a way to say no without hurting my feelings.* His stomach threatened an embarrassing eruption.

"Actually, Gabriel, I was out at Dad's place earlier, and I picked some sweet corn. His last planting is just right for eating, and my neighbors here in town gave me some tomatoes from their garden this morning. What would you think of coming over to my house for corn on the cob and BLTs instead? It's not as fancy as a restaurant, but we can do that another time."

Gabby sorted her words slowly, making sure he'd gotten them right. Corn on the cob. BLTs. Gwen's house. What did he think? *Heaven* is what he thought—that and a tumble of other things. "Sure," is all he said, though. Gabby didn't talk much.

978-0-595-40967-9
0-595-40967-9

Printed in the United States
71758LV00006B/220-231

9 780595 409679